CURSED DARKNESS

DUANE E. COFFILL

ISBN: 152331088X
ISBN 13: 9781523310883

9/17/19

For Madelyn, Savannah, and my beautiful wife, Shelley... I love you all.

To Jim,

Thank You!

[illegible signature]

AUTHOR'S NOTE

This is a revision of a 2008 published book. After years of being displeased with the original manuscript and the book's presentation, I decided it was time to do a revision.

A huge thank you to the New England Horror Writers. I had so much help and great advice that was given to me, I will truly cherish.

The first step in this revision was done by a Microsoft Plug-in called Grammarly. The final step was performed by S & L Editing. Their credentials are well known and I thank them for editing and revising my book. This book is the first of many that will be revised and re-edited. Thank you and I hope you enjoy this story as much as I enjoyed writing it.

Duane E. Coffill
January 30, 2016

CHAPTER 1

Tucker Falls

Tucker Falls, was a town of many residents and a lot of tourists. It was small, but filled with businesses, and a lot of money flowed in from outer towns. Mayor Anderson made sure the town remained small, unlike Freeport. Tradition mattered to him, and he wanted to keep it that way. Tucker Falls was a historic landmark.

In the 1600s, there were executions of many criminals, including murderers and rapists. There were twelve criminals executed in one morning. The first four were hanged. The second four were stabbed and their livers cut out; they died in agony. The last group of four was beheaded, and all twelve bodies were covered in salt and then buried, pig's blood used as their blankets. The townsfolk erected a big tombstone that read, "Those who were alive and in pain, are now in Hell with the Devil where their souls will BURN." Over the centuries, the exact locations of the graves were lost.

Johnny and Tracy were walking to school in their blue jeans, carrying their backpacks. A math test was on both of their minds, because they had studied the night before. Johnny's dark brown hair and slimness, like a Slim Jim, made Tracy feel unsure of herself, because of her slight chubbiness, but she was beautiful, like a rose. Jim and Tracy were both in the same grade. Tracy, with her hazel eyes and beautiful blond hair, held Johnny's hand on the way to math class. He held his head up, with false confidence, because he wasn't sure how he was going to do on the test. He sat down and there, in front of him, was the exam that would determine his future in college at USM. That was the question to be answered, and it would be answered, indeed. Tracy just walked into the classroom, and she too had her head up, as if she endorsed the feelings that Johnny was experiencing right now.

The test had over thirty questions: some were write-ins, and the others were multiple choices with three answers each. The test-takers had to guess which answer was the correct one. The math test lasted for about an hour and ten minutes.

The teacher, Mr. Briggs, collected the math papers, then brought them to his desk and sat down in his wooden chair. He examined the documents one by one, then looked at the clock and told the students to leave and go to their next class. *Of course, the dumb bell isn't working,* Mr. Briggs thought, *because the school figured the teachers can tell the students when it's time to go, but the truth is . . . this school is cheap!*

Johnny and Tracy walked holding hands, knowing that a lot of pressure had been relieved now that the test was over. There was nothing else they could do but wait until they found out exactly what they'd gotten for grades.

"How do you think you did?" Tracy asked.

"I hope I did all right. How about you?" Johnny asked with a starting glare at her. He was listening to her, but mostly he saw that she was stressed, and needed to relax.

"I think I did well. Probably an A or a B, hopefully," she said, looking into Johnny's eyes and getting lost in them.

"I think I probably got an A or a B as well," Johnny said with a smile.

"Anything's possible in this world of miracles. I prayed before I went to class, so hopefully I did all right." Tracy said, gripping Johnny's hand tightly.

"Do you ever think of the future?" Johnny asked, staring down at the floor and seeing specks of dust bunnies that were left over by the custodian, who used an unruly dust mop for the floors.

"In my mind, I wonder what it would like if we didn't have any more computers or cars, and especially sickness." Tracy was looking at her notebooks, then looked up to Johnny to see what his reaction would be.

"If there were no illness or computers in this world, everything would be wrong. Because our world is based on computers, and sickness will be around because it's been around since the beginning of time," Johnny explained to Tracy, feeling pretty smart because he felt that his answer was correct and logical.

No computers, no sickness, but what about drugs, crimes and corruption? Tracy thought, and she felt that Johnny was probably right, but deep down? Inside, he didn't care!

Johnny and Tracy walked away from the classroom, heading toward their next classes. They weren't in the same class, so they kissed and headed their separate ways.

Johnny sat in detention, writing away with his pencil on a math paper he had to do. He had some English as well, but that was all the homework he had, except the makeup paper. He pretty much knew what to do, so that would take him about ten minutes to write.

Tracy got home and decided to start right on her homework and see if she could finish early; that way she could have the rest of the night to herself.

Johnny kept looking at the clock: ten minutes left of detention, and then he would be home free.

Tracy had taken her last night hours ago; which was science and that was a breeze.

Johnny had earned his detention by swearing in homeroom, because the teacher wouldn't allow him to go to the bathroom. He hadn't really had to go—he was just bored.

Johnny went home to relax after three hours of detention. He was going to watch some TV and maybe give Tracy a call to see how she was doing.

Henry Joles was a man with a lot of his money invested in his house and farm. He didn't believe working for big money companies who promised a lot of things, but never kept to them. He was happier being with his animals and enjoyed the beauty of being his own boss. He worked whenever he wanted to; which meant getting up at five in the morning and calling it a day at three in the afternoon.

Henry Joles had his coffee and ate breakfast, which was three eggs and four pieces of toast with grape jelly. He had orange juice, and took his vitamins. At fifty-two, Henry believed one must eat well and take care of oneself to live a happy and healthy life, and maybe live a long life by honoring God.

Every morning, just before going downstairs to the kitchen, Henry thanked God for being alive, and then, after enduring his morning feast of vitamins and breakfast, he gave thanks again.

Henry stepped out of his house, walked to the barn, and opened the gate. He prepared the feed and got the food ready for his healthy farm animals. The morning was dim with the sun sneaking up on the horizon to his right. Henry was the kind of person who always thought mornings were the best moments of a day. Mornings always made him spirited and joyful.

The afternoons bored Henry. It took about two hours to do his rounds and chores when feeding the animals, and then he would walk around his field to see if there was anything on the ground that could hurt his livestock before turning on the electric fence and letting them out.

Henry was checking the field when he noticed dark rain clouds a couple of miles off in the distance, probably around the Pownal or Durham area.

Leaves were burning, and the smell was silky; Henry's neighbor was burning leaves because he forgot to do it a few days ago, and so he'd decided to do it and make the day a bright one.

Being a farmer had its traits, which meant it wasn't easy. You had to look after the farm, the property, the food for your animals and yourself; you also have to make sure your animals were in good shape and very healthy, otherwise they were useless and took time and food from more vigorous livestock. Otherwise, you had to settle with sickness, but sometimes that was okay.

It was three in the afternoon, and the dark clouds were rolling in pretty fast; especially since it seemed as if the clouds were aiming for Henry's farm. He said to himself and God, "We're in for a helluva thunderstorm." His thoughts were frightening and displeasing to his ears and mind.

As he returned to cutting grass by hand, as he had been doing since that morning, the storm was brewing with distant lightning and shallow thunder. The storm was coming, and it was going to be a nasty one! Henry started to gather up his animals and guide them into the barn. He was getting nervous, as the dark cloud was now completely hovering over his farm; he continued to guide his animals into the old red barn. He felt the breeze on his back, with thunder rolling above him as if God Himself hovered over the farm, and He was going to judge Henry as He'd judged mankind centuries ago when He flooded the earth, and had Noah guide only the good and build the ark. Henry was hurrying as the cloud started to spray its rage upon the farm. Hail smashed to the earth, and the windows of his house broke. His once- beautiful home was now going to be just a crappy white house with bad paint.

Henry finally got done, locked the barn and headed inside the house where he saw his kitchen windows, smashed to pieces along with his memories.

He made sure everything was locked tight so that nothing would come loose, and the storm continued to spend its rage against Henry's home and barn. It was seven in the evening when the storm moved on as Henry sat in the chair sleeping restlessly. He woke due to the silence that surrounded him. He had endured the storm with rage, but the concern was not for himself, but for his animals.

He went outside. The storm had destroyed his pickup truck, and every window on his home was smashed with dents from the hail that had tried to penetrate the house, but it stood tall and invincible against all odds. He looked outside; the cloud was still above him, but peace was within the dark cloud, the earlier rage gone.

Henry looked over his property. The barn was in good shape considering the power of the storm and what it had done to his house—perhaps to his pride as well. Farming was backbreaking work, and came with swollen hands and a stiff neck from his toiling and the stress of keeping the town off his back about taxes he owed. As he opened the gate wide, Henry found a big puddle of blood. The horse that had been there earlier was no longer in sight.

As Henry walked, he felt a drip on the back of his neck, and he started to feel strange in his stomach, as if he had eaten something that hadn't agreed with him. He turned to see if there were any tracks, but there were none. He continued to look around and kept feeling drops on his neck like rain. He figured that's all they were.

The horse was nowhere in sight, and it couldn't have taken off during the storm, because the barn was closed and locked. He started to look around, and he realized that the drips that have been dropping on his neck . . . were drops of blood.

His cast his gaze upward, trying to find the source of the blood.

Another drop fell on his forehead. With horror striking him down like an eighteen-wheeler, he saw his horse hanging lividly with its neck slashed from ear to ear. The blood was dripping from the large intestine that dangled, and there was green mucus all over, mixing with the blood. Henry had to pinch himself to see if he was dreaming or not, but the fact was . . . he wasn't!

The material used to hang the horse was metallic, but Henry had never seen anything like it. It was silver, like a sword, but oval, and the horse's head hung through its loop like a noose.

Henry was confused and scared as hell. He didn't know what had happened to his horse. A strange smell hit him like a wall, and he slowly turned to his right to see where the aroma was coming from. Henry saw all of his animals were torn apart, and blood was everywhere. He knelt over and vomited. He looked again and he threw up once more, and then he felt something sharp sliding down his back. The barn went pitch black and he heard breathing—but he knew his animals were all dead!

He knew something wasn't right. He felt something pierce his back, and blood gushed out. Henry screamed, but it didn't last. Blood sprayed all over the barn; suddenly there was silence.

The wind brushed through Tucker Falls like the ocean tide coming in from the deep sea, and the ships found their way to docking, thanks to the lighthouse that stood on the high hill just above the trees.

A fog bank was rolling in from the southeast, and the town was peaceful. The people who usually walked along the streets were inside their homes with their spouses and children. Daniel Tass was in his room reading a vampire novel. He was on page 136 of a 356-page book.

His gleaming blue eyes were set on each word and sentence; it was like he was trying to put himself in the book, which reading a story is all about. The slender body of Daniel lay on his bed with nerves that were motionless, and his mind was in a stalemate with the story.

The night had crawled up on the town, and shadows cast by streetlights fell over Parker Avenue and Hash Street. People in the town were very careful about strangers that came into Tucker Falls and didn't say much about who they were, why they were visiting, or how long they were planning to stay.

Those were some of the questions and many sayings in this small town of Tucker Falls.

I am one person that keeps to myself, but these people I speak of . . . are dear Ms. Howell—how I had such a crush on her and how badly I wanted to kiss her. There was one moment that I'll never forget . . . Daniel looked up from his book and saw the dark rain coming down, and decided to go find his cat, Harvey.

Harvey was found the next morning in a ditch near the home when Daniel's father was getting the mail. He thought he saw something out of the corner of his eye and turned to his left. He thought it was a skunk or raccoon, but it was Harvey. The cat was lying there with his tongue hanging out of his mouth.

Daniel's father was shocked, because Harvey looked like he had been torn apart by a wolf, but there were no tracks of any other animal except for Harvey. He knelt down, sad that this cat he'd known for so long was suddenly gone. Daniel's father knew his son would be upset about his cat.

He went inside to get a trash bag, and was going tell Daniel about Harvey, but he changed his mind. He didn't want to see his son hurt, and Daniel loved Harvey dearly. So he put Harvey into the trash bag, and then he got up and walked into the garage. He would bury the cat in the morning about three feet away from the house.

Daniel was a bright young 13-year-old with As in English, who wanted to be a writer someday. His parents told him that as long as he was focused and worked hard to accomplish his goals, he could do it.

Daniel was on page 210 in the novel, so he decided to take a break for a while and go fishing in the river. Daniel was walking through the shortcut he usually took because not only was it quicker, the neighborhood was much better to walk through anyway.

Excitement built in his stomach as he got closer, because there were a lot of good fish in the Androscoggin River, like bass, trout and pickerel. His eyes were focused straight ahead as he saw the river, and it was clear, moving smoothly and calmly, not like the rapids where one could fly fish and try to fight the current with all of one's might.

Daniel got his fishing rod ready. He tied a jig on and then cast into the water, hoping to nail a nice one. Daniel sat on a small hill overrun with trees. He sat there with his hands on the rod and a night crawler on his hook. *The jig just doesn't work at all. I was hoping it would do well for me, but the fish must know this lure pretty well, I guess.*

Two hours passed, and still Daniel had no luck at all. He was thinking about calling it quits, then suddenly he saw something jump from the corner of his eye. He quickly reeled in his line and cast over to the spot where the fish had jumped. He spun the reel slowly, and then felt a strong tug. He pulled the rod straight up toward him; then he knew had the fish on.

He was fighting with all of his might, and then the fish jumped, and it was a bass! He was excited because bass were damn good fish; they were even better when they were keepers, and soon Daniel was going to find out!

He kept the tension on as the bass was reeled in little by little. The reel made a zinging sound like a dirt bike. The fish was almost in, and then his line snapped! Daniel was shocked, like someone had stabbed him in the back with a lightning rod, but the fish he'd almost caught was now down under, laughing his ass off.

Daniel sat there on the hill in disbelief. He'd lost the big one; and a nice bass it would have been, too. It would have been great coming home and showing his parents what he'd caught.

Bad luck runs in many roads, and a lot of them lead to somewhere, but this one was a dead end. He told himself to get used to it and try again. *I should have had that fish. What's the matter with me? I should have set the hook quicker, or used another lure, or added twenty-pound test to my rod. That fish should have been mine.*

I'll get a fish!

Daniel kept fishing, and when he came home, he ate a ten-inch brown trout for dinner.

Johnny had spent hours at Tracy's house, and it was relaxing, because the storm had passed, but there was the talk of a rain shower around midnight. Johnny figured he would go home before nightfall, after watching a rerun of the *X-Files*. Johnny always enjoyed watching that show with Tracy, because of the endless possibilities of life from outer space or another dimension.

By 11 p.m., Johnny was home, and he had fallen asleep while listening to the radio with his headphones on.

It started to rain, and the fog rolled in. Soon the rain was coming down thick, as if it were sour cream and not water. As Johnny and his parents slept, there were cracking sounds on the roof, and then Johnny's bedroom window opened gently. A dark mist swirled into the room, and the radio died. A large shadow appeared in the hallway, and the hall light suddenly shattered into pieces. Johnny rolled over to his right side, and his headphones slid off. The curtains flew open and another shadow appeared. It to went into the hallway as if it were following the other shadow; and then the dark mist was gone, and the window was closed as before.

Blood spilled throughout the house as Johnny's family was slaughtered. The shadows came back into Johnny's room; in a flash, lightning lit up the scene, bouncing off the blood smeared on one of the shadow's mouths. The shadow licked its lips clean, and then there was nothing.

Johnny was dreaming of Tracy and making love to her on the beach in California. In his dream, Johnny was a stockbroker, and they had money. He owned his own business, while Tracy was a homemaker designing and selling crafts—and she was making pretty damn good money, too.

"Hi, baby," Johnny said.

"Hello, honey bunny," Tracy responded with a smile. She was wearing a bikini and she looked great!

"Seeing and making love to you is fantastic. I love you, Tracy."

"I love you too, Johnny. And I will always love you, forever and ever."

The town had suffered some casualties. Six murders occurred unexpectedly, and everyone was in a panic. The state police arrived along with the county police, and they blocked off everything so nobody could enter or exit Tucker Falls. Johnny was still asleep, but then his dream ended, and he woke up. The sun was shining through his bedroom window, and he slowly got up with food in mind. He put on his headphones just in time to hear the announcement that school had been canceled.

Everything was canceled. Johnny sat on the edge of his bed with his headphones on, shocked with everything had happened—and he was asleep the whole time! Fear caught in his throat,, and he started to get a cold chill down his back as he took off his headphones. He got up from his bed, and walked out of his room toward his parents' room. He saw lettering on the wall as he entered the room, and it read: MORE BLOOD WILL SPILL AS DARKNESS FALLS.

The words were written in blood, and he saw his parents were gone. His father's face was torn off and his heart had been ripped out of his body like a turkey on Thanksgiving Day.

Johnny looked at the ceiling and saw his mother. She was hanging from her large intestine that was wrapped around her throat. Johnny knelt down, and tears poured out of him. He cradled his father in his arms, and cried harder, like a child.

Tracy was brushing her hair. She had the radio on, and she heard the news about the murders. She sat on the closed toilet seat, shocked by the sudden episode. She ran over to the phone and called Johnny, but there was no answer. She ran downstairs, and as she approached her mother, Tracy saw she was crying. Tracy asked what happened, and her mother told her about Johnny's parents. Tracy cried, and her mother hugged her for ten minutes, even though it seemed like forever. "I'm sorry," Tracy's mother said while holding her.

"I hope Johnny is going to be all right, Mom."

Tracy held her mother tightly, and didn't want to let go, because of the loss that Johnny now would have to endure. "I'm going over to see if I can do anything for him," Tracy said.

"No, Tracy!" her mother said as Tracy ran out of the house. Tracy's mother sat down in her chair, and watched her daughter run, not sure she was going to be all right.

Tracy ran and ran as fast as she could. There were police over at Johnny's house, and she watched the morgue carrying out bodies. She stopped and wondered if Johnny was in one of those body bags.

Could she handle seeing his body, or bear the thought of losing him? Tracy decided to walk over very slowly, preparing herself for the worst.

Johnny walked outside, and she ran to him. He turned and he saw her, and then they met and they held each other tightly and tears poured down Johnny's face. Red spots appeared on his cheeks from all the crying he had done so far, and she was starting to get red spots, too. Together they cried, and he kissed her gently on the lips. She returned his kiss.

"Mom and Dad are gone. They're both dead!" Johnny said, pulling gently away from Tracy just enough to look into her eyes.

"I'm so sorry, Johnny. I want you to stay at my parents' house and . . ."

"No, I can't. I still have my grandparents, and they're going to need me now."

Tracy grabbed his hand and said, "We're sticking together—you got it?" She said it sharply, but with love.

"All right, you win, but I have a lot of things I have to do here, like get things and set up a funeral for my parents," he said.

"I'll help you with everything, okay?" she said, touching his pale face.

"All right," he said looking at her. He pulled her close and kissed her softly, and then they hugged again.

I can't believe my parents are gone! I loved them so much, and now they're gone, and I have no one except my grandparents and Tracy. I love her so much, and I won't let anything happen to her like I did with my parents."

The police were doing tests, and they questioned Johnny for twenty minutes while Tracy was at his side. They asked her questions as well, and then went back into the house. They continued to search for footprints and fingerprints, but the police wanted to make Johnny a suspect; in which he was, but it was a matter of time before they could prove that he had the motive to kill his parents and six other townspeople.

The sky filled with noise and bloodshed as Tucker Falls was no longer silent or a nice town to live in. It was now a town of despair, blood, and mystery, and along with that came . . . fear!

CHAPTER 2

THE STRANGER

I was in Bangor; many towns would call me the stranger based on my appearance and how I don't say much. I read in the newspaper about the murders in Tucker Falls. I was sad to hear people had died, but I knew that bloodshed would continue until I arrived, because I am the last of my kind.

I felt responsible for the killings in Tucker Falls, but I was not afraid to return there. I was just unsure if I could do anything for the small town. Fear was in mind as I hitchhiked to many towns and cities, but none were as strange as Tucker Falls . . . why?

The history of the town. The brutal executions that had taken place there three hundred years ago.

Walking the streets of Bangor, swaying my backpack, my clothes needed to be cleaned, as did I. I traveled outside Bangor, not too far from Old Town, and stayed at a motel called Hayes Inn; it seemed like a nice little motel. I paid the clerk for two days, then headed to Room 12, which was where I'd stay for the next two nights.

The motel was nice with fresh white paint and black trim, and the sign wasn't neon, like many hotels and motels that I'd stayed in all over the country, but had green lettering on a white background. The trees were close but nice. As I walked to my room, I looked out the window of the hallway and saw a dark cloud that I recognized from Tucker Falls. It was passing over the motel, and I saw gray spots appear just below it, as if the cloud had developed a disease, or skydivers were performing tricks for a show of some sort.

The spots disappeared quickly as the cloud hovered over the motel, and it seemed that it was heading south, perhaps back toward Tucker Falls and the Freeport area.

A cold feeling grew within me as I continued to walk to my room. Something inside told me that I was doing wrong; especially being up here and not down there where I should be, but how could I help them—the town? I stood in the hallway with my head down, and my backpack slowly sliding down my back as I thought to myself, I should be back there, helping the town; shit! I have no idea what I'm doing. I stood there wondering what I was going to do, then I realized that I should go down there and do my best to help them out.

The stranger left the motel that day to head back to Tucker Falls, the town with murder, mystery and a future of trouble. The stranger made his journey hoping to solve the murders of Tucker Falls. He knew he was the key.

He was hitchhiking on the Maine Turnpike, which was illegal and very dangerous considering that most drivers go about 75 to 90 miles per hour, going too fast and breaking the law.

The dark cloud had reached the town, and more murders were committed as the residents hid every time there was a cloud in the sky. The stranger knew he had to hurry, but he didn't know why.

He continued to walk, then hitchhiked due south, traveling the highway, figuring the state police would pick him up sooner or later.

The stranger was taken by a truck driver from Wal-Mart and he was heading toward Auburn, which was still a ways off from Tucker Falls, but would put him that much closer to his destination.

CHAPTER 3

THE RAIN PEOPLE

The rain was coming down lightly as the townspeople hid like rats in their homes, waiting for it to stop. They were scared and worried about the killer who only murdered when it rained; even during the day they would kill, though nighttime was their specialty.

A sudden wind came upon the town like fire rushing through fields, and the wind was strong, whipping the rain. On the edge of town where Jake's Cafe is located, shadows appeared, and they were dark and silent like a spider crawling on a sleeping body. The townspeople closed their shops, thinking *who would ever think a town would close due to rain, but it's happening. Tucker Falls is the town where the evil can kill at night, but it can die at daylight!*

Tucker Falls was hurting. Business was down and tourism was even lower. Only the townspeople would shop, and there were no tourists. They all stayed in Freeport and shopped around there, at places like the L. L. Bean retail store.

Tucker Falls had lost its business. The mayor was upset that his town would not grow due to the fact of these murders and the constant rain, and it never used to be that way. The rain continued its relentless horror as more citizens of Tucker Falls were slashed and diced in their very own homes. There was no hope, no place to hide and no way to fight something that couldn't be seen. Bloodshed fishing the river was part of Tucker Falls life and fun.

The Androscoggin River had importance, even though over the years, paper mills had polluted the once beautiful river. Now it was a river full of crap. The state was working to improve it, but for now, mills and other industrial factories continued dumping waste chemicals into the rivers of life.

Children were playing hide and seek while adults glared out through their windows with fear and terror of all the murders that had taken place in such a small town. Gordon and Will were two of children who were playing, and they ventured off onto Minor Street, around the corner from where they lived. Gordon's legs were skinny like chicken legs, but he didn't mind, because he felt he was fast as a cat and tougher than a junkyard dog.

Will was like a sumo wrestler. He was overweight and couldn't run worth shit, unless he was chasing after a burger. His parents pestered him about losing weight, and he tried, but it was impossible because he just craved food all the time! The boys were both eleven, and had been best friends since birth, some people would say.

They wandered into the night with mist at every corner and a cloud hovering over the city. Gordon and Will walked down Minor Street, talking about school and how hot lunches were now $2.25, and sometimes they were leftovers from the previous day.

As they were walking, talking about girls, and homework, and how much they hated school, a very foggy mist started to approach them. They stopped in their tracks and looked at the fog, wondering why it was moving at a rapid pace.

Gordon and Will started to walk backward, but they were cut off by more mist. They looked at each other and backed into the corner of the street.

"What do we do, Gordo?" Will asked, staring at the mist.

"We gotta run through it somehow, I guess," Gordon said, shaking scared and hoping he didn't wet his pants.

"Good plan, dipshit!" Will said with a shivering voice.

"Well, do you have a better plan, you idiot?" Gordon said.

"No. But I was hoping you did."

While the boys were against the corner of the street, they noticed the mist starting to disappear, until it was gone, leaving the rain behind. Gordon and Will felt like a couple of idiots thinking that the mist was coming after them.

The boys started to walk down Edward Avenue, the rain coming down very gently, until it began to come down fast, as if the sky was shooting bullets.

Gordon and Will ran underneath an overhang on a building to keep themselves dry. From around the corner, the mist returned, and this time it had light-red flashes in it, like there was a rescue going on, but no sirens.

Gordon saw this and jabbed Will. Will shook as the mist started to make its way over to them. They just stood there, wondering what was causing the strange flashes of red light. "Let's get outta here!" Gordon said, starting to run.

Will just stood there holding his pants and relieving himself. He ran out from underneath the overhang, but the mist surrounded him, trapping him. Gordon was halfway up the street before he turned to look and see if Will had followed, but he hadn't.

Will stood there trying to see through the mist, but it was impossible. Something grabbed his neck and lifted him from behind. Will was shouting in fear. Gordon looked on, too shocked to move; too scared to say anything. The being in the mist suddenly buried its claws into Will's back, and Will screamed as blood gushed out, and then there was silence.

Gordon stood there with his hands down by his waist, and saw his best friend being torn apart by something he couldn't see—but he did see one thing: his best friend's blood running down the street to the sewer. The mist started to move toward Gordon. Gordon started to run like crazy—he knew that his friend Will was dead, and he sure didn't feel like joining him.

Gordon ran blindly until he realized he was at the Tucker Falls Bridge. He was almost at the Durham town line, so he ran onto the bridge, which was small and only allowed one vehicle at a time because both towns were too cheap to build a bigger bridge.

As he ran, the mist was behind him. Gordon turned and saw something in the fog: it was Will's face, eyes blood red. The mist was gaining on Gordon, so he kept running, and then he jumped the town line. The mist started to follow him, but then stopped, as if it had hit a wall. To Gordon's surprise, it couldn't cross the town line.

Gordon waited ten minutes for the mist to disappear, then he slowly crossed the town line. For a moment, he felt safe, until suddenly, from behind, a claw grabbed his neck. He screamed and then there was a quick snap!

Gordon was dead.

Johnny sat in class with his hands on both sides of his head, thinking about Tracy and how she wanted to end their relationship after all this time. He felt like someone had crushed him, even though his family was dead, and he was living somewhere else. But Tracy was the person that made him happy.

His parents' funeral was three days ago, and he couldn't believe they were gone. Tracy almost had broken up with him while the murders in Tucker Falls became more and more gruesome with every killing, and the police had no clues or suspects.

Johnny wondered beyond his mind's expectations, and thought how he had lost his parents and now Tracy was next for him to lose. The stress of teenage life had its ups and downs, but this one reached all the way to hell!

He wondered why Tracy had broken up with him; even though they had problems, they had worked things out, and everything should have been all right, but things weren't and Johnny had to find out what happened to him and Tracy.

He walked out of class after his math test, which had been difficult because of all the things that had happened to him. He wondered why life was so hard for him right now; everyone had problems, but all at once? He was walking down the hallway when he saw Tracy at her locker. He wanted to approach her, but he didn't know what to say except *Why did you break up with me?* He'd asked that question millions of times in his head, but he couldn't approach her.

As Johnny walked slowly past her, Tracy turned her head, and as she watched him, her eyes welled with tears of guilt. She felt so bad breaking up with Johnny, because he was truly good to her, but she was scared, and she didn't know what to do but end her relationship with Johnny and focus on school—and not on the murders that everyone was talking about.

She turned away and faced her locker, closing it, and she went to class while crying.

Johnny went to his class depressed, and he too developed tears, but not much, because he didn't want anyone to see him crying or else they would call him a *pussy*. Days had passed, and the killings still continued, and Tucker Falls was now under alert.

The townspeople had closed their businesses early and school let out at noon, not 2:30 p.m. as it was before. Johnny and Tracy finally agreed to see each other, and they talked by the Androscoggin River for three hours.

"Johnny, I'm so sorry for breaking up with you. I don't know what I was thinking, but please forgive me," Tracy said, looking into Johnny's eyes for forgiveness.

"I love you, Tracy. Why did you break it up with me? I thought everything was good between us; especially with my parents gone and I'm living with my grandparents and helping them around the house. Why did you do it?" Johnny asked, looking at her beautiful hair as she gazed into the river, looking for an answer that would soothe his broken heart.

But she didn't have a reason—she just did out of fear. "I was just scared, that's all, Johnny. I'm so sorry for everything that has happened to you. I love you very much, but what I did was wrong, and again, I'm sorry." Johnny looked at her, hoping she would turn her head and look into his eyes, and then she did, and he saw that she meant everything she said. But he also saw that she was a little lost based on everything that had happened in Tucker Falls, and between them, too.

Johnny and Tracy looked at each other and hugged, and held each other very tightly, and nothing could have broken their grips on each other. As they were doing this, the river ran smoothly, and the night was approaching.

Night had fallen, and the dark cloud hovered again over the town of Tucker Falls again. It was raining heavily; everyone was inside their cozy houses and they watched and locked their doors while waiting for something or someone to get killed.

The mayor had the town police making routine patrols throughout parts of Tucker Falls, and every child was locked behind doors. Couples embraced each other, holding and protecting their loved ones.

That night, nothing happened. The next day the town reported no murders, and everyone was shocked. In the next couple of weeks, no murders took place, but ten cats were ripped apart, and dogs were also sacrificed. Humans were spared, but their guardians were taken out and torn apart as if they had been made of paper.

The night came again, and the rain fell once more. Shadows walked the streets of Tucker Falls looking for something—something to kill, to rip apart with sharp razor-like teeth, and eat the flesh like turkey on Thanksgiving.

Tracy and Johnny were walking with their hands entwined and smiles on their faces. That morning, Johnny had bought her flowers to show how much he loved her. When he'd gotten to her house she'd still been sleeping, but her mother had woken her to tell her Johnny was there. She'd gotten up, gone to the door, and he gave the flowers. She'd embraced him with one eye open, being half asleep, because it was Saturday morning. She had been hoping to sleep in, but that wasn't the case at all.

After they had hugged, she stood back, and he told her how much she meant to him. She'd started to cry, and jumped up in the air with her arms wide open and he caught her, but he lost his balance. They both landed on the cold, wet ground with her on top, knocking the wind out of him.

That day, Johnny and Tracy walked all over town holding hands and giving each other hugs and kisses. But the town had suffered another loss in their community—a ten-year-old boy. It was Will.

The police had no clues, and no witnesses; which meant no leads. Chief Charles Barnes was at the scene of the crime. He had his police officers doing everything in their power to try and find some clues or even fingerprints.

Chief Charles Barnes was thirty-six, with a scar on his right cheek from a knife fight he'd had five years earlier with a killer in North Carolina. He'd been trying to arrest someone suspected of breaking into older peoples' houses, killing them, then stealing everything in sight. The suspect turned out to be the killer, and he pulled a knife on Barnes. Other officers rushed to the scene and saw the killer ready to take out Barnes. The suspect was shot and killed, and Charles Barnes was made chief of police three years later in Tucker Falls, Maine.

Chief Barnes was walking around, glancing at the victim, and he just knew this murder was related to the other deaths that had happened over the past few months. He didn't know who was doing these sick killings, but in his mind, he was going to find out who it was, sooner or later.

Johnny and Tracy inadvertently walked to the scene of the crime, where a police officer told them they had to stay back behind a yellow ribbon. The police officer's silver badge flashed brightly as the sunlight hit it at certain angles, making it flash.

Johnny saw the blood smeared on the tar, and Tracy had her head in Johnny's arms. The sight of blood made her sick to her stomach, and she wanted to throw up. Will's liver had been ripped out, his stomach leaked blood and green fluid from its inner walls, and his intestines were overlapping Will's face as if he were playing hide and seek, but that wasn't the case at all.

The arms of the victim had been bitten or ripped off. There were bites and claw marks all over the body; it was like a pack of wolves had torn up Will.

Johnny couldn't help watching the blood that splattered every time one of the police officers tried to move the body to look for clues, but sometimes that didn't work either. Fear had conquered Will, but in life many things did—like many people were afraid of unusual circumstances, such as things that lived under the bed, or behind a closed door, and you can't see what's behind it; especially trying to sleep at night, but you're too afraid to sleep, because you're scared that you're going to be dragged underneath the bed and eaten alive by a hideous monster.

That was Tracy's fear; she kept it to herself because she thought Johnny might make fun of her, or worse, laugh at her.

Chief Barnes examined the body with a latex glove he was wearing on his left hand, and picked up a small piece of black cloth that no one else had seen. The black piece of cloth had been under the victim's right arm—or what was left of it.

He gave it to a detective to have it checked out. Chief Barnes spotted Johnny and Tracy, who were still standing next to the yellow ribbon. *I wish these kids would learn to stay away from a murder scene. No wonder this fucking country is going to hell—because of stupid kids like those, watching us checking the scene for clues.*

Chief Barnes decided to walk over to them and say something. "Hey, you guys shouldn't be near this area—it's a bad spot to see such a terrible thing," the Chief said with caution in his voice.

"I know, Chief; we shouldn't be here, but the victim was a kid we knew, and he didn't live very far from me." Johnny explained.

"I know you knew him, but we want to know who did it, and why they had to do such terrible acts of aggression and kill this kid beyond death." Chief Barnes felt horrible that this kid's future was taken away from him by some monster, or maybe a cult of Satanists looking for a small sacrifice.

Johnny, Tracy, and Chief Barnes talked for fifteen minutes. Chief Barnes had to go to the boy's house and tell his parents that their son, Will, was dead. That was the part of the job that made Chief Barnes sometimes wonder why he was in this kind of work.

The murder scene eventually cleared, and all the townspeople stood there throwing daisies onto the scene and they bowed their heads. Pastor Kile Dims said a prayer for the dead boy, and they all prayed for the murders to stop and let this town have its peace and let them go on with their lives.

"Please God, let us live and be peaceful with each other. Stop this murderous rampage that is happening in this small town of Tucker Falls. We ask of you, Lord Jesus Christ our Savior, please save us and please forgive us of all the sins we might have done that would cause such evil to kill our friendly community, one by one."

The townspeople prayed and held hands while this was going on. Johnny and Tracy were walking home. Chief Barnes had offered them a ride, but they turned him down, as they wanted to walk to Johnny's house together. Tracy would stay the night, but Johnny would sleep on the couch while Tracy took his bed—that was the deal he had with his grandparents.

The rest of the town prayed until dawn came, then everyone went home to try and go on with their lives.

The stranger was sleeping in Kay's Motel on Route 100 in Waterville, next to Oakland. He was having bad dreams about Tucker Falls: he saw the victims, and they came alive and asked him, *Why did you let us die? We didn't deserve to die!* In the dream, Will and Gordon were playing with their soccer ball, but it was Gordon's head that was being used for the shot.

The drifter woke up in the middle of the night, sweating and crying from the all bad things he had seen in his dreams: but how was he related? He moved his golden cross that was loosely around his neck was something he gotten when he was younger. It showed Jesus on the cross and there were gold petals on each of the cross. It was a little worn. According to his mother, it had been in the family for centuries. The chain that held the cross had been cleaned numerous times over the years and the stranger felt it was good luck.

He got out of bed and walked over to the bathroom, which was the size of a closet. He turned on the water faucet and started to wash his face, as if he was washing away his sins, or the bad things people would do or say to each other. His sin was leaving the town and living his life like an ordinary person, but he knew he couldn't do that now.

He felt as if he were connected with the murders that had taken place in Tucker Falls and he wanted to do something about it, but he didn't know what to do, except go back to the town. He was heading in the right direction. After he had washed his face of all the sins and the evil things he'd been experiencing in his dreams, he got down onto his knees and begged for forgiveness from the Lord. After he had done that, he got up and went back to bed. He fell asleep knowing what he had seen: he had to hurry and get back to Tucker Falls before it was too late.

CHAPTER 4

FORGOTTEN

Wayne Lewis had murdered his wife, Dorri, for cheating on him. He was heading for Tucker Falls, hoping to forget that he had just bashed his wife's head in with a hammer; he'd smashed her with it about twelve times, and then she was dead.

He was coming up from Sanford, and he'd decided to hide out. His wife's lover had had an accident with some poison in his drink the night before. Dorri found out about it when Wayne told his wife he'd done it and she'd threatened to go to the police. He took this under advisement and killed her.

He thought about turning himself in, but the media would've had a field day with him. They might even make up an even crazier story of their own, or twist things around a little bit to draw ratings to their stations.

Wayne was tall and thin, and he had a slight southern accent from his youth in Charlotte, North Carolina. He was very wealthy, owning his own cleaning company, *Wayne's Train,* which offered cleaning with a lot of custodians and floor specialists who buffed and maintained particular hardwood, brick, tile and stone floors for customers. His service was popular with businesses and people who didn't have time to clean, because either they worked too much or were just too busy with other activities. Wayne had had his own business since 1983, and it started out with just him and wife right out of high school, which meant he'd never had time to attend college. He'd proven that he was able to do it—but he couldn't by himself; Dorri had helped.

Wayne was still wearing his black suit, with a white shirt underneath, and he wore a black tie that Dorri had given him at Christmas time. He drove his '99 Plymouth Breeze into town, and noticed there was no one outside, which was odd; it was only 8:30 at night, but all the lights were off, and all the small businesses were closed.

He drove around looking for a motel or somewhere to stay the night, but everything was closed. He knew he had to stop somewhere and gather his thoughts. He wished he had stayed somewhere in Portland or Freeport, but the police would probably check those areas. He'd wanted to try and find something small, but comfortable, and Tucker Falls was the only place that had come to mind.

He thought about going somewhere else, but killing two people in two days takes a lot out of a man. He decided to try and find a back road where he could park the car and sleep in the backseat, then head out in the morning.

He saw a sign for Omar Road, and he turned down it slowly. It was a dirt road with potholes, and he sure didn't need a flat tire. *I'm glad I killed the bitch and her pussy lover—they deserved to die, and dead they are. What a weird feeling; killing two people and then making a run for it and gathering thoughts on my story for the fucking police, that it was her lover that killed her and then he killed himself just to be with Dorri in the afterlife . . . yeah, they're both in Hell now!* Wayne pulled the car over to the side of the road, and he put it into park and shut it off. He stepped outside and urinated on the ground—he'd been holding it since Sanford, almost wetting himself while killing Dorri. *Ahhhh, what a relief. That felt good.*

God, I'm glad she's dead. Oops, I got some on my slacks. Shit! What a moron I am sometimes!

Wayne finished what he was doing, zipped up his zipper, and got back inside his car. It was getting chilly outside, but he had a warm jacket that he'd brought, just in case he needed it.

He was in the backseat of his Plymouth, laid across the seat as if he were home in bed. As he lay there, he started to think about all the times Dorri and he'd had together, the good and the bad, but, of course, that was history now, thanks to Mr. Lewis.

It was 12:30 a.m. and Wayne's car was covered with frost, but surprisingly, he wasn't cold at all; even though he'd been dozing off and on for two hours now. He'd been trying to work out the details of what he'd tell the cops—he had to get his story exactly right, or else his ass was finished. Wayne kept staring at his watch, and then a gentle rain started to fall, like smooth ice melting from the top of a roof.

The rain was relaxing, and Wayne dozed off again, until the rain was gushing down as if the fire department was spraying their hoses all over Wayne's car. He was startled awake when something bumped his car, as if someone had banged his bumper with a cart from Shop N' Save. He quickly noticed his car was shaking from front to back. He glanced around to see if someone was playing a joke, like the old urban legend with a body hanging from a noose bumping gently against the car as the person in the car waits for their companion to come back, but they don't—instead they are being watched by a serial killer.

Wayne thought about that urban legend, but then came to his senses and figured it was just the rain.

That rainy night, Bobbi Paul was walking the back roads of Tucker Falls, a sixteen-year-old who was suspended for beating up another girl. She was dressed in dark Lee jeans, and a jean jacket, with a Godsmack t-shirt underneath it.

Bobbi lived with her parents and an older sister, Maria, who was a senior at Tucker Falls High School. Bobbi walked a good threc miles from her house; she'd had an argument with her parents about the fight she got suspended for. She'd once had a crush on Johnny, but he told her straight out he loved Tracy and not her. Bobbi had slapped Johnny and then walked off while Johnny stood there with a red mark on his left cheek where he was just hit by a girl. Rumors got around about Bobbi and Johnny—people were claiming they were going out—but Tracy knew the truth: that it was Bobbi who had started those rumors, just to get back at Johnny. She hated Tracy with a passion, just for the fact that she had Johnny and Bobbi didn't!

Bobbi walked down Omar Road with the rain hitting her roughly like it was attacking her. She noticed a car with Maine plates parked by the side of the road; she knew almost everyone in town, but this car she had never seen before. *What's that car doing there, unless a couple of people are making out or doing the thing? Hmm . . . maybe I should peek and see what they're doing.* Bobbi walked over to the car, fighting the rain, and she didn't mind the weather, but maybe she could find some shelter for the moment. As she got closer, she noticed there were dents all over the car, and holes in it, as if someone had poked into the car with a crowbar or something.

Bobbi was cautious about the car, because even the windshield had been cracked. She tried to look inside the car, but didn't see anything. Suddenly, from behind, a hand grabbed her. It was Wayne; he had been stabbed numerous times, and was gushing blood from his mouth and stomach. "Run!" he said, holding onto Bobbi's arms, and blood splattered her jacket. She pushed him away, and he fell to the ground as if he couldn't walk or had no legs.

He looked up at her and repeated, "Run!" His eyes were filling with blood, and the rain was falling heavily—it was like salt hitting his open wounds, and he screamed a little from the pain, then fell back and died. Bobbi just stood there, her eyes wide, as if she had seen her father doing drugs. Wayne Lewis just *died*, and she started to get some ideas. She knelt down and checked his pockets. She found his wallet with two hundred dollars, so she pocketed the cash and put the wallet back into his pocket. She started to run; she was heading home, knowing that she'd just stolen money from a dead man who'd told her to *run*—and run she did.

She ran very fast, hoping to see her house any second, but suddenly she tripped and fell, scraping her left knee. It was bleeding a little, and she looked to see what she'd tripped over, and it was a dead cat.

She walked over to the cat with her eyes glued to its carcass, because there was something else, but what? As she stood over the cat, she heard squishing sounds, so she knelt down to examine the cat closer, and she saw maggots and tiny worms slithering around in the intestines. She turned away, holding her mouth, trying to keep herself from vomiting, but her throat got tight and then BOOM! She threw up on the road, then once more and she said to herself, *well there goes dinner. Boy what a waste of time this was . . . I'm here throwing up over a dead cat, and I should be home in bed sleeping and feeling pretty good, but of course, dumb old me; I have to be a rebel about everything.*

Bobbi got up and started to run back home again, but something grabbed her leg. She tripped and banged her knee on the old tar road a second time. She looked around, swearing up a storm, and vowed to kill whomever had tripped her and that they were in for a big surprise. She got up slowly, holding her right knee, and the pain was indeed intense; it was almost to the point where she couldn't walk, but she kept moving and her leg seemed to get better. Her home was just around the corner. She limped along, and then from behind, a boy's voice spoke to her.

"Don't go, Bobbi. Stay and play with me." Bobbi turned around, but she didn't see anyone. "Play with me, Bobbi," the voice said again from the darkness.

"Where are you, little boy? Are you in trouble? Or are you and your friends playing a fucking trick on me?" Bobbi asked, hoping to get a response from someone who could be playing a sick joke.

Bobbi glanced into the darkness, the rain hitting her gently, and she felt as if someone were watching her. She started to walk backward toward home, but turned quickly when she spotted something ahead of her in the middle of the road. She peered, squinting into the thin dark air to get a better look, and then she gasped as she felt herself being lifted from behind. She was thrown into the woods, landing on the wet ground with a hard thud. As she shook her head to gather her senses, Bobbi heard something shuffling through the bushes toward her. She attempted to get up, but her left leg was bruised or broken, she crawled through the tall bushes, fallen branches in her way and drops of rain splashing her as she ruffled through bush after bush. "Please God, let me live and get home," she prayed.

She begged and then she had to stop, the throbbing in her leg unbearable. She gripped her calf as a sharp pain shot up through her knee. The shuffling sound was closer. Bobbi crouched behind some small bushes and tried not to say anything or move, even though the pain felt like a bunch of needles sticking into her whole leg. The bushes trembled as something walked through them and the noise got closer and closer, and then stopped. Bobbi sat frozen on the wet mucky ground, holding her leg, trying to ease the pain. In one quick motion, she was ripped from the bushes she was hiding behind, and she screamed in terror. Bobbi felt multiple hot stabs pierce her body: she couldn't breathe, and felt wetness coming from within. She felt weaker, and then cold claws gripped her and shredded her into pieces and then . . . she was dead.

Chief Barnes was at the scene where Wayne was found dead, less than a half a mile away from where Bobbi's body had been discovered. The sky was gray from three months of gloominess brought by the dark cloud that hung over the town, dishing out misery to all the towns-people. He stood there with sickness growing within him, knowing there were no clues, no suspects, and no witnesses. *These murders must stop! Every time I come to a crime scene, it's always the same thing, someone who is innocent, but this one is different. What was it about this time that would bring such bloodshed to a small and beautiful, peaceful town like Tucker Falls?*

Officer Hughes was checking out a torn piece of black cloth that had been hanging on a bush. He put on his latex gloves and slowly pulled the cloth off, placing it carefully into an evidence bag. He spotted Chief Barnes and started to walk over to him. "Chief. Chief? I found something." Deputy Hughes yelled, hoping to get Chief Barnes's attention. Chief Barnes heard Hughes and met him over by Bobbi's body. "Chief, I found this piece of cloth from a bush that was about halfway between the two crime scenes. It looks ripped to me, what about you?" Hughes gave Chief Barnes the baggie, and Chief Barnes held it up while Hughes looked at him hoping to get approval from his boss. Chief Barnes stood there in the tall grass and gave it back to the deputy and told him to have it tested. The officer knew he did well because the look that Chief Barnes gave him was a positive one and not a "you dumb shit" look.

Officer Hughes got into his squad car and drove off to the lab, hoping to find some form of evidence on it like fingerprints or DNA from the murderers who got scratched or cut from one of the victims fighting back. Chief Barnes stood on the road, looking up into the sky, searching for answers, but there were no answers, just riddles.

What kills at night when it rains and what walks through the rain looking for victims? Answer: the Rain People, that's who! Chief Barnes shook his head at his own nonsense answer.

Johnny and Tracy were camping by Miller's Brook, which was a few miles from town. Nobody was around, no cars, and no fisherman because the brook itself had microscopic in it based on the events that had been taking place in the last few months. The sun was out, and it was nice and warm with some flies still out in the fall climate. Johnny glanced at the sky and watched as an ominous cloud formed over Tucker Falls, and the sky started to fill with darkness. The warm, sunny day was now gone. The downpour started without warning. Johnny and Tracy scrambled to pack up their things and hide underneath a big oak for shelter. They watched the rain come down like crazy, as if it were possessed. It was very thick, like bullets, but more diaphanous. The rain sliced through branches; small trees were being shredded like cottage cheese. Johnny and Tracy knew if they walked into the rain, there was a real possibility that they too would get shredded, so they stayed put to wait out the storm.

The rain was coming down heavily, and the sky was darkening with a mist, but there were white dots in the mist as if something were directing the rain and fog like a conductor. Johnny and Tracy sat underneath the big tree that remained stable the throughout the massive hail of rain bullets. They sat there with hope, holding each other and embracing their deepest thoughts and fears; which seemed to be happening right now in front of their eyes. The two teenagers held each other tightly, staring into the dark rain of blades. There were streaks of redness in the sky like a rainbow that appears after it rains and the sun pops up intensely. The redness was dazzling like the sun, but a little shady. Then, without warning, the rain stopped, and the sun came out. A rainbow appeared, but it had something in it that a rainbow shouldn't have: the color black.

"That's weird. I thought rainbows just have colors, and not a black stripe?" Johnny asked, staring at the odd phenomenon.

"I thought so, too, but there it is," Tracy said in awe, looking at the strange rainbow as well.

"Wow! That's weird. The rainbow's fading, but the black is still there in the sky," Johnny said with disbelief.

"Well, anything is possible, I guess in this world of the unusual," Tracy said. *I guess there are some things I just don't know anything about,* she thought.

"Do you think that black strip is somehow related the murders, Tracy?" Johnny asked, still staring at the sky.

"I don't know, honey. Maybe this whole situation does have something to do with murders, but how?" Tracy put her arms around Johnny's waist as if looking for protection and comfort from him. Johnny didn't say anything.

He was reticent when he thought about his family and how he missed them. He wanted to know who killed them. He had kept his emotions about his murdered family deep within him, but now he felt like he was losing control of everything. He'd almost lost Tracy; he did lose his parents; he was lucky that his grandparents loved him and had taken him in, but the loss of his parents still hurt him very much.

Johnny turned away from Tracy as he started to cry. She came over to him and put her right arm around him to comfort him. She knew what was going through his mind at that moment, though she couldn't know how bad it was hurting him because she still had her family. "Johnny. Are you all right?" she asked, looking up at him. Johnny turned toward her, wiping his tears away, trying to be strong, because he didn't want Tracy to think he was weak or anything.

Johnny squeezed Tracy tight, because although he was in pain, he loved her. "Johnny, are you going to be all right?" she asked with concern, stroking his hair gently. He enjoyed her doing this, because it made him feel good, but also it was a way of her telling him that she was there for him.

"I'll be fine. What are your thoughts on what happened today?" he asked, looking into her eyes and seeing she did care for him.

"It was something very unusual. But what should we do about it?"

"I think we should tell the Chief and see what he says," Johnny said, letting go of her and focusing on the task at hand.

"All right. Sounds good to me. Let's tell him; even though he might think we're crazy, let's do it."

The two teenagers collected their things and headed back to town. Hopefully Chief Barnes would believe them, otherwise the word would get around that they saw a UFO or God gave them a sign or something.

CHAPTER 5

Death Comes to You

Wanda Nook was a thirty-three-year-old waitress working at Hillman's Pub, making $4.00 an hour plus tips. She had been a resident of Tucker Falls all her life and she started to work at Hillman's Pub when she was 18. Not much of a life, but she liked her job; even though her dream was to be an author, writing romance novels, but time and her imagination seemed to have dried up, and the ideas had run out.

She hated the job, but choices were limited in Tucker Falls: either you worked at York's Mill, Lazy Laundry or as a waiter or waitress. She thought about leaving town, or finding another job outside of Tucker Falls, but towns like Brunswick and Freeport weren't exactly looking for waitstaff, because everyone who already lived in those towns got the jobs first. She could never understand this, but things worked out that way; especially at places like Friendly's, which was an excellent restaurant to work at, she'd heard; but again, you needed to live in town. She applied for these jobs based on experience from the job she had right now, but she never even got a phone call or had an interview set up. Wanda would work eight nine-hour shifts to pay for rent in Wings Apartments, which was $325 a month plus utilities.

Wanda's shift ended at nine, and she headed home, driving her '87 Ford Escort, which needed a new muffler. She didn't have the money to cover it. She was driving into town when it started to rain. She wanted get to home as quickly as possible, especially with the two murders that had taken place in the past few days. Usually when it rained, flooding was a problem, but not tonight. Wanda was trying to figure out why. As she drove, she thought about work and how depressing it was to make so little for all she did, but there were times she made $200 in tips on a good night, and that was sweet!

She still wanted to be a writer. There were things inside her that couldn't be explained except by putting it on paper; even if she wasn't a very famous writer, she'd like to be successful, just enough to write full time. That was her dream. Wanda thought about all this as she did every time after getting out of work. *I wish I were a full-time writer. I'd be good; I know I'd be a great writer. Writing romance novels and making some cash—and maybe a movie deal as well! Oh, my, that would be nice, instead of this life of making less money doing more, and having guys whistling and asking me to come home with them.*

Wanda was paper thin with ocean eyes and a green light of a personality. Her childhood was very good because both of her parents had provided well for her; she was an only child and they'd kind of spoiled her, but they also disciplined her as well. Wanda wondered why it was so hard to write a story; even a three-page story was hard. She often got depressed about herself and having no friends; she had friends at work, but they were just associates. She had tried to get together with a few people, even going out with a few dishwashers, but they were losers, and she really wasn't interested in spending time with her coworkers outside of the job.

She drove into the parking lot at Wings Apartments. She lived in number 45, on the second story of the second building. There were three buildings in all, and the parking lot was big; especially having

50 people including friends and family over all the time, you needed that extra room. She went into the building, climbed the stairs to her place, unlocked the door, and went inside. Wanda threw her things down and flopped onto her couch with her feet hurting from being on them for nine hours, and most of the time without a break and just a few bites of food and a few drinks of Sprite or Cola. *Oh, what a relief. I love being home; working at that damn place all day and having no freaking breaks except to go to the bathroom or get some or to drink something. Why do I live my life this way? What a fool I am. I have so many other things I want to do, but where do I start? Oh please, God. I need some help with my life. I want a better life for myself, please God! Help me!*

Wanda fell asleep after fifteen minutes, and she still had her uniform on, a white shirt with a black tie, and a red skirt. She dreamt about tomorrow because it was her day off. She dreamt of finding another job, but in all of her dreams, it was raining. It was as if she was walking through town and it was raining, and she could see her parents waving to her and she would run to them. Then they'd back into an alley and she would follow them; but as she got to the entrance, there she saw her parents ripped apart by a shadow. Its eyes filled with blood, staring at her with pieces of flesh hanging off its claws, and it would start to come toward her and she would back off and try to run, but she was surrounded by these dark, horrific creatures in the rain. She screamed for help, but no one was around and then one of them would grab her right as she woke up. Wanda woke in a pool of sweat from the terror she'd endured in her sleep. She was tired, but needed a shower and some TV; she liked to watch *M*A*S*H* on TNN.

She got her clothes ready, then went into the bathroom and turned the shower on. She let the water run for a few minutes so the hot water could kick on, because she loved it hot; it relaxed her. After the shower, she dried herself off, pulled on her Winnie the Pooh jammies, and went into the kitchen to get dinner ready. She was making spaghetti with meatballs, her favorite. She added the pasta to a pot of boiling water, and went into the living room to sit down while waiting for the spaghetti to cook. She turned the channel, and there were reports of another killing in Tucker Falls and the State Police were coming in and taking over the investigation. *Well, it's about time the state came in; hope their investigation isn't as useless as our police department is right now.*

Wanda wished these murders would stop, but they seemed to be getting worse, and Channel 8 had newsperson Chuck Jones on the scene.

"I'm Chuck Jones, and I'm at the scene of another gruesome murder in Tucker Falls, where five-year-old Paula Roy was murdered the same way as the other victims." Chuck stood in front of the camera with sunfish hair and his chocolate eyes eyeing the camera; Wanda thought he was kind of cute, but he had an ego—a very big ego! *Boy, he is cute. I would love have him over for dinner and maybe a little nappy time. No, he would never go out with a waitress like me who only makes one tenth of what he probably makes. He'd look at me as if I were some low-life or scumbag or something in that league.*

Wanda stared at the tube, watching Chuck do his thing, and then she shuffled back into the kitchen, drained her pasta, and prepared dinner for one. She sat down and ate her meal all by her lonesome. It was midnight. The town was quiet, with a little drizzle, and everyone was asleep. They'd wake up in the morning to the news about another murder taking place in Tucker Falls. Wanda was sleeping heavily, the same dream occurring over and over. The dream felt very real; even though her parents had passed away five years ago in a plane crash on their way to Florida. The plane's right engine had caught fire, and they crashed in Georgia, and all of the passengers on the plane died.

That was probably the most difficult time in Wanda's life she'd had to endure. She'd had some cousins and relatives around to share in her loss, but Wanda was hurt the most because those were her parents, and now they were gone. She'd had recurring bad dreams about visualizing the plane crash and how she wished she could have done something about it; but she knew it was impossible to stop a plane crash unless you were God.

There were no murders whatsoever that night. It was a big relief for everyone in town, but it didn't mean anything; it had happened before where there were stretches when murders didn't take place for a couple of nights, but they always picked up afterward.

Wanda had just had an argument with her boss, Ted. She walked out on him while he was yelling and screaming, and all the customers heard him, and they too walked out—his language had been pretty offensive. The restaurant was empty with the exception of a few employees who were still around because they needed the job. Wanda left the building crying, and drove out of the parking lot squealing her tires while Ted looked out the window, watching her leave.

That fucking dick! How could he be so bad? I didn't mean to be late by ten minutes. My car wouldn't start; how could he yell at me like that? That fucking . . . dink! Wanda was very upset, and when she got home, she threw her things inside her apartment and pitched herself onto her couch, wondering what she was going to do next.

The stress and the yelling made her sleepy, and she was out like a light; even though she was dreaming about her parents again, she relaxed and enjoyed the fond memories of her beloved mother and father. At two o'clock in the morning, there was a knock on her door. Wanda remained asleep. The knocking at the door became an insistent pounding, and Mrs. Lowell, Wanda's next door neighbor, woke up, disturbed by the hammering at Wanda's door. She got up and opened her door and then suddenly, Mrs. Lowell was no more.

The next morning, Wanda woke up from a long, comfortable sleep and opened her door. She screamed at the sight of Mrs. Lowell torn apart, blood splattered all over her doormat and Mrs. Lowell's door as well. The walls and floor were covered with blood. Wanda accidentally stepped in a small pool and it smeared on the sole of her foot. Wanda glanced at the slaughtered woman, then ran to her other neighbor's apartment, and they called the police. Wanda was crying, because Mrs. Lowell was like a mother to her. She was there for her every time she had a problem or something was on her mind, and also they would get together quite a bit too.

The police were at the scene while the coroner awaited permission to take care of the remains of Mrs. Lowell.

"Did you see what happened here?" a distant voice asked Wanda while she was in the parking lot, crying. Wanda turned to see who it was asking the question. "Well, did you see what happened?" It was Chief Barnes. She looked at him, wiping tears from her pale face.

"No, I didn't see anything, sir," she said, wiping the remaining tears from her eyes and trying to gain her composure.

He took out a handkerchief and handed it to her. "Thank you, sir," Wanda said, passing the handkerchief back to Chief Barnes, damper now due to her tears. He looked at her, and he saw the pain in her face and he knew she felt worse for Mrs. Lowell than the other people nearby, because they weren't crying nearly as much as Wanda.

"Ma'am, can you tell me if you saw what happened here?"

"No, sir, I didn't see anything, but Mrs. Lowell was like a mother to me, and her and I spent a lot of time together. She was always there for me, because my real parents died in a plane crash a while back, so she kinda took over." Wanda continued to cry, and Chief Barnes offered his handkerchief again, but she kindly refused, and just wiped them away with the back of her hand.

"I'm sorry to hear that, ma'am. But I need to ask you a few questions, because I'm sure you've heard about all the murders that have been taken place in the last few months."

Wanda nodded. "Yes, I've heard about the murders, but I . . ." Wanda started to cry harder and Chief Barnes handed her his handkerchief, and she took it this time. "Thank you, sir," she murmured.

"Well, did you see anyone or hear anything last night?" Chief Barnes asked, looking uncomfortable.

"No, I didn't see or hear anything, sir," she said.

"I can't believe that no one heard anything at last night, especially any kind of sound or her yelling for help." There was frustration in his voice. "The same thing has been happening over and over, and with no clues or fingerprints."

"I understand you're upset, but she was like a mother to me, all right?" Wanda retorted.

"Ma'am, I'm just looking for answers, that's all," Chief Barnes said, looking at Wanda's red eyes. He saw anger there, but he also saw fear and someone with a lot of problems. "Ma'am, was there anyone outside when you were home?" Chief Barnes asked.

"No. There wasn't."

The Chief finished with the investigation within an hour after talking with everyone and gaining little information about what had happened there. Chief Barnes went back to his car and sat there with his finger on his lip, trying to gather his thoughts on the murders, but again, he was clueless.

Wanda went back into her apartment, disoriented, and thought of what Chief Barnes had asked her. She felt a little more worried based on a number of questions he had asked her; he had no idea who was doing the killing. She went into her bedroom, threw herself onto her cozy comforter, and, due to the emotions of the morning, found herself dozing off.

Chief Barnes left the crime scene, thinking of all the possible clues to this murder. *God! This damn murder has me up in arms and sometime soon I'll have ulcers from this case. I'll end up fat, and my favorite food will be donuts or McDonald's or something. I must think. This case can't be too complicated; I have enough experience to solve it, but what's going down and who the hell is committing these murders? Fuck! I sure don't know!*

Chief Barnes went back to the police station. He walked in and headed over to his office, slamming the door and waking the other police officers who were asleep at their desks. He sat down in his old squeaky chair and glared at the coffee-stained desk. He was trying to come up with some ideas, but it was useless. He'd made this case his personal mission; he had detectives, but they lacked experience, and he wanted to take this case head-on. But he couldn't seem to find any answers.

Mayor Thomas Anderson was forty and glancing at himself in the wall mirror across from his desk. He was admiring his baldness that shone brightly in the sun and fluorescent lights hitting his head from all angles. *I'm a great mayor! This town is nothing without me.*

The mayor was pleased, because after the initial scare of the murders, when businesses had shut down and tourists had stayed away, there had been a recent influx of thrill-seekers and novice detectives that had been morbidly curious about Tucker Falls. *These damn murders have caused a lot of pain, but at the same time money is rolling in with tourists taking pictures of our town. I hope these murders will last a little longer—but not into next fall, when election time rolls around again. I need to have this town safe and in perfect shape before I run again. If we can find the killer right before the next election, I'll be all set!*

Mayor Anderson had been mayor for six years, and a lot of townspeople thought he was an honest politician, but everyone knows that politicians are out for themselves and not for the American people. He sat behind his desk with his brand new computer that he'd just got from Dell, and he was surfing the net looking for different sites to check out. That's how he spent his time, surfing the net or going home to take a nap and then waking up and heading back to the office. He was a distant relative from the first settlers. His ancestor was Judge Holden. He was responsible for handling criminals and a lot were guilty before innocent; especially if some kind of witchcraft was used. He died horribly with Hornets in his mouth and maggots had refuge in his rectum. But how? No one knew. It was all of sudden during a storm with a dark cloud over the town and it rained heavily for three days, leading up to flooding and a five more deaths occurred those three days.

Tracy woke up in a cold sweat, the leaves outside drumming against the window by her bed. The wind was howling as fall was gone and winter was here, but there was no snow, just chillier temperatures, enough for it to rain and thunder. Tracy sat up on her bed and thought about the murders; she'd dreamt she was killed by something in the rain, but she wasn't sure what it was, only that it was dark and frigid.

She got up and looked at the clock: 2 a.m. She had no school the next day, because the school was closed down temporarily. Three kids had stayed after school last week, and they were found dead outside the gym. The school board had decided to close all schools in Tucker Falls until further notice—which meant until the murders had stopped and the killers were caught or killed. Tracy had known those kids. They'd been in her science class.

She looked out the window and saw a stranger walking the street. He stopped and looked up, as if staring directly at her. She was startled and backed away into the darkness. She continued to watch the stranger, who stood outside looking up at her. She was afraid that he was the one doing the killing. She closed her eyes briefly, and he was gone.

Her heart was pounding like drums during a war dance. She glanced out into the street, looking for the stranger, but he was nowhere to be seen. She went into the kitchen to pour herself a glass of Coke to settle her nerves, and then returned to her bedroom. She put the glass on her nightstand with a half of glass of soda still in it. Eventually she fell back to sleep and dreamt the same dream: her death.

Johnny dreamt the same dream as well. He saw Tracy in his dream, and he tried to protect her, but it was too late. He saw her death and then he saw his death, and he woke up suddenly in a cold sweat, his sheets wet with fear.

He got up from his bed and wondered about the dreams he'd been having of these shadows or dark people with red eyes that keep glaring at him. They'd attack over and over, with the same ending: he'd get killed! Johnny went into the living room, and he sat down to gather his thoughts. He thought about Tracy and how she was doing, and wondering if she too was having bad dreams.

Johnny fell asleep on the couch in the living room, and he dreamt once again the same dream and he died the same way. He woke up in small pool of blood. He looked around, panicked, and saw bodies hanging everywhere with fresh blood dripping, and there was one word, written all over the wall: RAIN, RAIN, RAIN. Johnny was scared, and pinched himself, hoping this was still a dream and that he would wake up. He kept pinching himself until he bled, and then he saw the doorway that led outside, and it was raining out. Johnny saw fire-red eyes glaring at him as if he was trespassing, or that he might be dinner. He looked around to see that he was surrounded by these people with their fire eyes, and he couldn't say a word or even move.

Behind one of the rain people, he saw Tracy hanging from a tree. She had been gutted, and her blood was splattered all over the ground. One of the rain people said, "Johnnnnnyyy." The thing's voice was harsh and dark, and Johnny looked at the thing and screamed, and then they jumped him!

He woke up falling off the couch, and realized that it had been another bad dream, but to him it had seemed very real. He thought about the experience he just endured, and he knew there was something in the rain that was evil. There was something in the rain that would kill every time it did rain.

A hand grabbed his shoulder, and Johnny jumped. "Ahhhh! Oh, it's just you, Grandpa," Johnny said with relief.

"What are you doing up, John?" Grandpa asked, putting in his false teeth.

"I had a nightmare. These people were in my dream trying to kill Tracy and me."

"Well, bad dreams can sometimes be signs of the future. My father told me that back when I was your age, even though I don't consider myself ancient—but I'm no damn James Dean, either!" his grandfather said. Johnny looked at his grandfather and knew the man that stood in front of him was a proud man. He had worked at the shipyard for many years, though he and Grandma had enjoyed their retirement ever since. "Are you in some trouble, John?"

"No, Grandpa, I'm not in any trouble. These murders are just so close, and losing my parents and . . ." Johnny started to cry, and his grandfather pulled him close and held him in his arms, and he felt the pain within Johnny. He shared that pain, from losing his family as well.

Johnny and his grandfather stayed up for another hour, and then both of them went to bed. Johnny dreamt the same dream over and over, as much as Tracy did.

The next October marked a year since the murders had begun. Johnny and Tracy were still together, and the town of Tucker Falls still felt the threat of the killings, but the murders had slowed down for the summer and things had slowly slipped into a routine . . . until now. The leaves were turning pretty rainbow colors, and the trees turned grayer with cold falling upon the town. During the hot summer, the rain had all but stopped, which left the town in somewhat of a drought. There had been only four murders during the entire summer season. This was very unusual, because the killings were happening almost daily until that time. Tucker Falls at the moment was experiencing a boom, with tourists crowding the town with people and money; which Mayor Anderson loved very much: dollars!

At the Tucker Falls Inn, there was a visitor staying there, and he went by the name of Harley Drift. In other towns, Harley had only been known as the stranger.

He was the talk of the town, and he had arrived last winter and worked as a custodian at the Tucker Falls High School. He worked second shift. The pay wasn't great—only $9.50 an hour—but Harley was happy to be working again. *I was hoping to find a decent apartment, but found nothing. I've been fortunate to be able to stay at the Tucker Falls Inn for this long time. It also helps that my relative was murdered, and I got some money from his will, being his last remaining family.*

Staying at the Tucker Falls Inn was excellent and only cost a hundred dollars a week, but it didn't include meals. That's how the stranger was able to afford to stay there, along with his recent inheritance; he was doing well for himself.

The stranger was cleaning one of the patios at the high school when a dark chill ran down his back, and he looked up at the sky. He saw that trouble was coming, and he knew that this time, they would find out the truth. Harley Drift went back inside the school. He had five hours to go on his shift, and he thought about the dark cloud he'd seen coming from the west. He continued to sweep the classrooms using a small dust mop. Ronny Jordan, one of the students, came to the door and asked, "Would be all right if I got my books?" Harley nodded, continuing to sweep. Ronny came into the classroom, walked over to his desk, and grabbed his books. He offered Harley a quick "thanks" and left.

Ronny was seventeen, a junior in high school, with a grade average of B+. He was not an athlete, but a student with a great interest in computers and books. He lived on Marley Street, a few blocks from the high school, and Ronny would walk it every day with his nose stuck in a book.

It was raining heavily, and the sky was dark gray. Harley saw this and wondered what was going to happen. He remembered being in Bangor around this time many years ago, and going from building to building and city to city in the years since. But this time felt different. Harley was shaken from his thoughts by screams coming from the end of the hallway, near one of the exits. He ran out and spotted Ronny being pulled outside by something he couldn't see. Whatever it was had a hold of Ronny's leg, but Harley couldn't make out what it was, because the rain was thick and the sky was dark gray.

Harley ran down the hallway toward Ronny, and grabbed him by both arms. Harley found himself in a tug-of-war with the unseen force. Ronny screamed out, "Harley, don't let go! I can't free myself; it feels like something is ripping my leg apart! HELLLLP . . ."

Suddenly Ronny was pulled with great force, and he disappeared into the rain. Harley fell to his knees due to the strength of that final pull, and he saw Ronny's face vanish into the storm. Moments later, blood splattered all the doors and windows. Harley was soaked in Ronny's blood, and he caught a glimpse of yellow eyes in the rain. Something reached out for him, and he shut the doors on the thing's hands. He watched in horror as Ronny's screams faded, and then there was nothing. Ronny was dead and Harley the stranger couldn't do anything about it.

Harley sat on the tile floor and looked outside. The sky started to clear, and he saw the sun begin to set, earlier now at the beginning of fall. He'd never seen someone die or be murdered in front of him. A teacher ran down the hallway and saw Harley sitting on the tile floor, covered with blood, and she spotted books on the floor. As she moved closer and passed Harley, she looked outside the doors and saw Ronny's body—or what was left of it. She screamed and ran down to the principal's office and called for help.

Harley just sat there, wondering about Ronny and how he'd just come in and asked him for his books, and before he knew it, Ronny was in trouble and Harley was trying to save him. *What did I do wrong? Oh, Lord. I am so sorry. Ronny, I'm so sorry for you, guy. What the fuck happened? Who or what the hell was that?*

When the sirens were right outside the school, the principal and the teacher came down the hallway to meet the police. Chief Barnes came down the hallway and gave Harley a stern look. Then he concentrated on the body and the teacher, Ms. Edward, and the principal, John Wise, glanced at the body and then they turned their attentions to Harley; who was still sitting on the tile floor covered in blood. Harley was in shock. Chief Barnes walked over and knelt down in front of him.

"So, what's your name, sir?" Chief Barnes asked gently, trying to remain calm. Harley looked at him and didn't answer. There was an emptiness in his eyes, and Chief Barnes saw this, but he had a job to do, and he was going to do it. "Sir, what's your name?" Chief Barnes repeated, with more force this time. Harley didn't answer; he didn't say anything, but instead stared at the tile floor while the blood on him started to dry.

Chief Barnes was getting frustrated with Harley, and then the principal spoke up and said, “His name is Harley Drift, he was the stranger that left town last year and decided to come back to Tucker Falls to settle down.” Principal Wise was looking at Harley and feeling kind of sorry for him.

“All right, Mr. Drift. What happened here?” Chief Barnes said, but Harley wouldn’t even look at the chief. “Mr. Drift, what did you see?” Chief Barnes was raising his voice, and he studied Harley. He knew Harley was either in shock or hiding something, and he wasn’t going to say a word. “All right, you want to play this game? Let’s go down to the police station and I’ll ask one more time, and then, if you don’t talk, we’re going have some trouble!” Chief Barnes said, getting up and shaking his head in disgust. Chief Barnes called his troops, who were at the end of the school, and two uniformed officers came over. Chief Barnes ordered them to take Harley down to the station, which they did without handcuffs.

“Do you think he’s the one who has been doing all the killings, Chief?” Ms. Edward asked, watching the two policemen take Harley down the hallway and out through the front entrance. They put him gently into a squad car and drove off to the police station. Chief Barnes ignored Ms. Edward’s question. He shook hands with Principal Wise and Ms. Edward and thanked them for their cooperation. Chief Barnes left while Principal Wise and Ms. Edward were leaving as well. In the meantime, the coroner had shown up along with two forensic techs, and they took care of the crime scene.

Harley was riding in the backseat of the squad car with the two police officers. Harley was thinking that the police might blame him for the murders, because he was a drifter in a lot of ways; especially traveling and moving and never staying in one place for a long time. He knew there was something wrong with the town, but he couldn't put his finger on it. What he saw today, though, scared the hell out of him.

It was raining again, and the windshield wipers went back and forth, and Harley felt that the police were going to try to pin the murders on him; it was a gut feeling. Harley looked out the window of the squad car, and he saw images of the thing in the rain and how they had killed the boy. *Those bastards! How can they kill such a young man? The police are going to blame me somehow, but I wasn't responsible at all. But they were looking for the right opening to nail someone; especially a stranger like me. Who or what were those things in the rain that killed that boy and tried to get me? That poor boy.*

The rain was coming down heavily by the time they reached the police station. Chief Barnes arrived about five minutes after the two policemen walked Harley into a room for questioning. "Chief, The mayor wants you and Mr. Drift to go over to the town hall and meet with him," the deputy said while hanging up the CB.

"Oh, you're kidding, right?" Chief Barnes said angrily.

"No, Chief. The mayor wants to meet him, but he only wants you and Mr. Drift to go over alone, and not me." The deputy looked over the chief's shoulder, where Harley was sitting with a concerned look on his face. "It sounded to me like the mayor wants to give our killer here a piece of his mind."

"Fine. We'll head over now. I'll contact you later when we leave the town hall," Chief Barnes said. Chief Barnes had control over certain situations, but in the chief's contract with the town, it stated that Mayor Anderson had control over the Chief. Chief Barnes never knew why, but it was in his contract. The two drove off while the deputy watched.

CHAPTER 6

Little Evil

George Landers was driving in the heavy rain that pounded his front windshield. He was two miles from Tucker Falls, and the sky was growing dark as nighttime approached. He was coming home from a business trip he'd had in Boston for a bubble gum ad, and the deal had worked out; he was going to make $100,000 from it, and to him that was sweet. He was fifty, making great money, and he had a nice home on Rural Avenue, which was the only house on that road. George was divorced and had no relatives: the closest friend he had was Mayor Anderson. He had been in a car accident ten years ago with his sister, who was always seen holding a doll and she died from the car accident. George had been devastated every since and blamed himself, because it had raining that night and he lost control of his vehicle and he went off the road and hit a tree head on. Another driver had been coming the other way and the car was always all over the place and George hit his brakes quickly and she was killed instantly. When he came to, her doll was gone and he never who was the other driver that caused him to swerve and drive off the road. She was only nine.

He was driving his Ford Taurus, which was his go-to car for business trips. He drove it a lot, but he also had an old Mustang in the garage, and he usually drove that on the weekends; it was his pleasure ride, and he took good care of it as well.

The deal worked out great. I can't believe that I'm going to make that much money on one deal, but they're royalties as well and boy, that's going to be sweet! Maybe I'll retire in a couple of years; hopefully unlike those other deals that fell through, this deal is sealed, and the check is supposed to be in the mail by Tuesday. God loves me, boy, God loves me . . .

George Landers enjoyed being a businessman. It was his style as a sales person, the way to sell and seal deals was his thing; even though he'd had his fair share of bad deals in the past, somehow he always made up for his losses. He was almost at the Tucker Falls Bridge separating Tucker Falls and Durham, and he saw something in the middle of bridge. He stopped his car, but the rain was pouring down and he couldn't say exactly what was on the road. He got out of his car and started to walk over to the object, and he saw a little girl holding a pink purse. She was drenched to the bone and just standing there on the bridge, holding her little pink purse. She glared at George. She wore a baby blue dress with a white t-shirt underneath, and she had dark, long brown hair and cherry red slippers. She looked for all the world like Dorothy from *The Wizard Of Oz.*

George couldn't believe what he was seeing, and he approached her and asked, "What are doing here? And why are you out in this mess?" He knelt down and tried to listen, but she didn't say anything. She just stood there looking at George with an odd stare, as if she'd seen a ghost or something. He asked her one more time, and she didn't respond, so he took her arm and guided her back to his car. He helped her in and buckled her up. He was surprised that she went with him, and didn't even say a word. He sat there with his car running, and he studied her as she sat with her pink purse and her seat belt on. He wondered what was wrong with her. He turned to her and asked, "Where are your mommy and daddy, little girl?"

She said nothing. She didn't even look at him, just glared into the rain still pounding on the windshield. He repeated the question, but still she said nothing. He turned to look forward, thinking of what he was going to do. He decided to head to the town hall; maybe the mayor would know what to do, because sometimes he worked late. As George drove over the bridge speculating on what this little girl was doing out in this mess, he kept stealing glances at her. She just sat there with her head facing forward watching the trees go by, not even blinking. George wondered how could anyone not blink, but then she did blink, and he continued his short journey. When he pulled in, he noticed two young people; they looked like teenagers, and they were heading for the town hall, too. There was a cruiser already there and George wondered what was going on. He stopped in the parking lot and turned to the little girl, who was sitting quietly, and said, "Well, we're here, and we must go inside and find out what the mayor might be able to do with you. And hopefully, find your parents or whoever takes care of you." George got out of his car and heard the passenger door open, and the little girl was getting out, too.

George went around to the front of his car; the little girl was already there waiting, holding out her hand while watching him with those dark cold eyes. Then she smiled at him, and he smiled back in surprise, and they started walking toward the town hall. They climbed the old wooden stairs and George opened the door for her. She walked in and he followed, and they headed for the mayor's office, which was down the hallway.

The town hall was fifty years old and had been rebuilt a few times. Back in the early 1800s, there had been a fire, and the town hall had been completely destroyed. The cause of the fire was never known, and then the same thing happened in the mid-1900s. This time a lightning strike caused the fire, and the people of Tucker Falls had declared it a sign from God which meant He was angry with them; then three months later that notion was dismissed, and the town called it *an accident.* The parking lot was small, with enough room to fit about twelve cars, and when the lot was full, you had to park on the street, which meant maybe walking a mile or so, because of all the tourists that were always in town admiring the history of Tucker Falls.

George and the little girl walked down the hallway looking at pictures of past mayors and old photos of the town hall being rebuilt. They got to the center floor of the town hall; it was the size of a small cafeteria, and took up so much room, that's why the parking lot wasn't that big. George saw the mayor talking with the two teenagers, Chief Barnes, and the chief had someone with him who looked unusual. George went over to the mayor, still holding the girl's soft hand.

The mayor's office was full of people talking and yelling about what had been happening in town. Mayor Anderson was trying to calm everyone down. Some of them walked out in frustration, while Chief Barnes and Harley Drift remained, along with Johnny and Tracy, Mayor Anderson's secretary, Lilly, and George and the little girl. The eight people that remained jumped when lightning struck the flagpole flying the American flag. Everyone ran to the nearest window, and they looked out and saw the flag burning in front of their eyes. The flagpole tilted, then fell with a bang like a cannon going off. Mayor Anderson hung his head as if shamed. The rain picked up again, and suddenly there were loud screams throughout the town; the screams could be heard from a mile away. The people in the town hall stood there near the windows glancing out like school children looking out waiting for it to stop raining so they can go outside and play. George turned to the mayor and said, "I have a little girl here, and she's not saying a word where she's from."

"Why are you telling me this? I'm not the damn police, you know!" the mayor said bluntly. Chief Barnes looked at Mayor Anderson. *You son of a bitch! What a cold-hearted piece of crap you are! I can't believe I voted for you. Man, what was I thinking . . . hell, I should've ran for mayor myself and probably could have been elected before this son of a bitch!*

The eight people walked back near the center of the aisle and looked at each other as the power flickered on and off like someone was playing with a light switch.

The town hall did have a backup generator, located out back in a small shed. "Well, what the hell is going on here?" Mayor Anderson asked, throwing his arms up in the air.

"Mr. Mayor, Tracy and I believe that there's something wrong with this town—something unknown," Johnny said. He could see disbelief in the mayor's eyes, but he wanted to say it anyway. Johnny and Tracy were looking at the mayor, and they saw that he was, in fact, terrified.

"Now, hold on. I still have this little girl here who doesn't speak, and I don't know what to do," George said. He was still holding the little girl's hand. She showed no emotion.

"Well, just hang on here, there's other town business going on first, and then I'll deal with your problem next, all right?" Mayor Anderson asked George, who nodded.

Mayor Anderson walked around the office with his head down. He was thinking about all of the problems that were mounting before him, and he decided to sit down behind his desk and have everyone come in and put their heads together in the hope of finding answers.

"Mr. Mayor, there's something wrong in Tucker Falls, and it's not natural!" Tracy said.

"What problem are you talking about, Tracy?" the mayor asked.

"The killings in this town are not caused by anyone, but by . . . some *thing*!" She described the black rainbow she and Johnny had seen. She hoped no one would yell at her or call her stupid.

"She's right, Mr. Mayor," Chief Barnes said. He'd had a grip on Harley's elbow this whole time, but now he let go and he stepped forward, next to Tracy. He knew she was right, and that's why the police had not been able to catch the perpetrators that had killed so many town folks.

The mayor sat in his chair listening to statements from Johnny, Tracy, Chief Barnes, and then another voice spoke.

"Sir, I'm somehow responsible for these murders in this town," Harley said; he was unsure of how to continue, waiting for Chief Barnes to take him back into custody, but there was no such reaction. Harley had everyone's attention, except the mayor's!

"Now, if I remember right, you ran off up north to live on the road, right, Mr. Drift?" Mayor Anderson said, his finger pointing accusingly at Harley.

"You're right. I did run away, but I'm back because there's something about what's going on here that has to do with me. I don't know how, but I'm somehow responsible." Harley slammed his fist on the mayor's desk, trying to show he was serious.

The mayor looked at him curiously. "Well, if this is true, then how do you intend to cure this problem we're enduring right now?" The mayor was open to suggestions. Harley stood there on the carpet with his hands to his sides and no answers. Everyone in the room became quiet, the only noise being the rain coming down heavily on the old rooftop of the town hall. Suddenly, a dark mist funneled down from the sky and the town hall was surrounded by a thick fog. The outside world was invisible, and all the doors that led outside clicked.

Man, we're in for some trouble! Why in the hell did this have to happen to me during my time as mayor? God, sometimes I ask myself that question: why can't things go my way at least once . . . why? Mayor Anderson's thoughts were profound and truthful as he and the seven other individuals said nothing, all thinking, but now the terror was around them, and they were trapped.

Chief Barnes tried the telephones as the CB wasn't working, and Johnny and Tracy with Harley tried the exits, but it was no good: every door was somehow locked or being held tightly from the outside. They tried to break the windows, but something made the glass sturdy and unbreakable.

CHAPTER 7

The Hidden

The rain came down slowly, as if there were a war going on outside along with the thunder, but there was no lightning, just a very strange dark mist trapping them inside the town hall with no communication with the outside world. They prayed that they would all make it out alive. Tucker Falls was swallowed by a cloth of darkness as the gloomy mist that surrounded the town hall expanded around the town, and everyone was trapped in their homes like laboratory mice in a maze of confusion. For those who were on the streets, in their vehicles or walking the night, this once peaceful town was now a town on the alert. But some didn't care whatsoever about the killings, such Jamie Joy and her boyfriend, Ted, who were making out in the backseat of his car near the high school. They were just making out: she was a virgin and he was not.

He wanted to go all the way because they'd been dating for six months, and he figured it was time to take things to the next level, but she was still not ready. "Cut it out!" Jamie cried as Ted reached for her buttocks, and she shoved him off her. They sat in the backseat with the windows fogged up and they both looked out on separate sides.

Man, she has a great-looking body. I would love to score with her, but she just wants to save herself for later; I don't why, because I do care for her, but love her . . . I don't! Ted sat there in the backseat next to her, fully erect and hoping she was thinking about changing her mind.

But this had happened many times before, and they'd just kiss and make up and drive away. *Why does he get so fresh with me? I'm not ready yet. He should know this by now, but why does he still try to get it on with me?* Jamie wondered if he only wanted sex, and didn't love her.

"Jamie, what's the matter?" Ted asked as he looked at her longingly, and she was still looking out the window with thoughts flowing through her mind, wondering what the truth was.

"Ted, you know what's wrong. You do this every time we get together: you want to go somewhere and talk and every time, you pressure me to have sex!" she shouted, tears rolled down her bright cheeks. He'd lost his erection, and he reached out to gently touch her shoulder, but she brushed his hand away. He shrugged and got out of the car and into the dark rain. Jamie sat there in tears, her Slim-Jim body wet from when Ted opened the door and the rain came pouring into the car. She sat there, not feeling the rain, thinking that maybe Ted did love her, but how would she know? Ted was her third boyfriend, and the other two had tried the same—one had even tried to rape her. But Ted had come along and kicked the shit out of him, and that's how they'd met.

Her golden hair and blue eyes were dripping with rain, and her face was covered with her salty tears. Ted walked around in the rain, getting soaked to the bone. He kept pacing back and forth, hoping to come up with something that would convince her that he cared about her. He didn't love her, though. He was hoping if they had sex, he would fall in love with her, and she would love him back. Ted thought she did love him, but she was scared, though because making love sometimes would either make two people one or it would split them completely and love would no longer exist, only lust. Ted kept walking back and forth, thinking about what to say to her while gallons of water dropped on him within minutes, and he decided to tell her the truth. It was the right thing to do, even though the truth might hurt her, but it might finally get her to agree to have sex with him; that was, if she would still be with him.

He headed back to the car, but he couldn't find it. He kept looking for the lights that he'd left on when he and Jamie went into the back seat to talk. *Where is the hell that damn car? Shit! I know I left it right around here. I thought I left it right here?* Ted kept walking, then he realized he was nowhere close, trying to see in the darkness of the mist. It was nighttime, but when he'd gotten out of the car it hadn't been that dark at all, because the moonlight had brightened the land. But a dark cloud had come in and shut out all the moonlight. Ted searched for his car so he could apologize to Jamie for being a jerk and always wanting to have his way with her. He knew she wasn't ready for sex; maybe later on.

Jamie sat in the car trying to compose herself. It was getting a little chilly, so she climbed over the seats, turned the car on, and set the heat up on high. *God, where's Ted? I need him with me. I'm getting scared being out here, and Ted just walked off mad. Well, the hell with him! I can survive without him; especially if he only wants to have sex with me and that's it . . . well, he's in trouble!*

Ted kept walking into the dark mist that was light like regular fog, but there was something different about this mist; it was still raining heavily, and there was a fog bank. Ted was asking himself many questions when he saw what looked like a campfire, but strangely, it appeared to be near the school. He walked toward the light, covering his head with his hands. When he got to the light, it was a campfire, though the rain should have prevented it from burning so brightly. Ted wasn't sure what was going on. He stood watching the fire, mesmerized. From behind him he heard branches breaking, and he turned quickly and saw something staring at him. He was trying to focus on the woods that were in front of him, and he heard another snap, and he suddenly felt helpless and he yelled out, "Hello, is there anyone out there?" The rain had begun to slow, and he tried to squint through the drizzle to make out what was there, and saw something shifting behind the two trees in front of him. He looked on the ground for a thick branch that he might use as a weapon, and he picked one up and he held it tightly, waving it like a gladiator waiting for a battle.

"You're alone, boy!" The voice was dark and misty.

"Well, come and get it, tough guy!" Ted shouted, and then he screamed, and the rain picked up once more.

Jamie had started the car, but it stalled. She tried it again and again, but couldn't get it going. She sat in the driver's seat with her hands to her face, hoping Ted would be back soon because she was frightened and it was pretty dark outside. *Ted, where the hell are you? Man, it's freaking scary out here; especially being all by myself and I have no fucking clue where Ted is . . . . Please come back soon, Ted? I love you.* She did love him, but love had nothing to do with it right now: it was all fear.

Jamie decided to sit in the car and wait for her boyfriend to return. Jamie was getting worried, and decided to hit the horn, hoping to draw him closer. *Maybe he's lost or something? I don't know what to do but sit here and wait for him. I don't even know how the hell I am going to get out of here with all this darkness around me and this mist that smudges the windshield.* Jamie was terrified that Ted was either lost, or he was pissed off and had decided to leave her alone and never see her again. But if that was the case . . . how would he get his car back from her if she did decide to take off and go home? Jamie was thinking of all kinds of possibilities that could have occurred.

The mist continued its rally against the car. Smudges of images were appearing on the windows. Jamie saw something moving around in the heavy drizzle, and turned on the lights to get a better look. It was hard to tell what was there, because the mist was hard to see through, but there was something moving around outside. Jamie tried the car again, but it was dead.

She sat in the car with tears rolling down her cheeks, holding herself and hoping that was Ted outside, playing games with her. Something brushed up against the car, as if someone had leaned against it for a second and then gotten off. Jamie looked around, trying to see who or what had done it, but there was no one. She sat, trying to pierce the foggy mist, and suddenly another movement bumped the car. She screamed a little, echoing inside the car.

She thought about what to do, but she was in shock, and then something else brushed against the car. She screamed again, then jumped in the back, crawling over the front seats and hitting her head on the ceiling and landing hard into the backseat where Ted had many times tried to talk his way into Jamie's red fury of passion. She lay there with her feet barely touching the other end of the car, holding her hands next to her untouched breasts, and prayed to God that everything would be all right. Something else banged into the car, but it was done heavily, like a massive man leaning against it and then pushing himself off.

Thunder arose around her as something pushed against the car, rocking it with force, as if another car were gently pushing Ted's car into the unknown. *Please stop! I beg you! Please stop! I just want to live and see my parents and hope for Ted to be back soon. Please, God, help me!* The pushing stopped, and Jamie wondered what happened. She arose slowly and looked out through the back passenger window. To her relief, she saw Ted looking back at her, standing there with his wet shirt and jeans. He was waving for her to come out, so Jamie crawled over into the driver's side and she pushed the door handle and began to open it. It took her a moment to realize that half of Ted's body was missing! She reached to quickly shut the door, but something grabbed a hold of her and she was sucked into the rain. There were screams of pain—but there were also screams of joy, the sick screams of a madman who kills for pleasure, who laughs and then screams because the killing overcomes him and he becomes insane. And Jamie was dead, and her body would never be found.

CHAPTER 8

Do Not Fear The Rain

Johnny and Tracy were sitting together in the conference room while everyone else in different areas in the town hall were trying to gain a sense of the current situation and how they were trapped by something that lives and kills in the rain. They all wondered what was going to happen to them if they tried to escape. One thing could happen: they could all die!

Johnny had his arms wrapped around Tracy like a blanket, and she was shivering with fear; he was too, but he was burying it within himself and trying not upset Tracy more than she already was. He wondered how this would turn out. Would the rain ever stop and would the sun ever show up again? It was the midnight hour, and the sound of rain coming down was heavy at times, but then there were sounds of people walking on the roof as if they were looking for a way in. Johnny was trying to figure things when the power went out. Screams rang throughout town hall, and then the emergency lights came on and everyone calmed down, their heart rates slowing after that short and sharp fear.

The little girl was by herself in the corner of the office, just standing there with her eyes gleaming at everyone. She wondered what everyone was thinking about what was happening. Mayor Anderson was asleep, with his head flat on his desk. He had removed some of his paperwork to get comfortable. Others were still awake, waiting for daylight, but it seemed that the night was far from over. Chief Barnes was with Harley Drift, and he knew now that Mr. Drift was not guilty, but he was helpless, having no control of the current situation.

The secretary was found dead in the bathroom; she'd slit her wrists with a steak knife, and there was a message on the wall near the toilet where her helpless body lay limp. The message read, ONE DOWN, SIX TO GO! BEWARE THE RAIN! Chief Barnes had found the body, and now there were six of them left. It appeared that she had killed herself, but why the message? ? Mayor Anderson was awakened by George, and he ran into the bathroom and saw her body.

"What was her name, Mr. Mayor?" Johnny asked, while holding Tracy in his arms. She was distraught with the sight in front of her.

"Her name was Lilly Peters, and she was one of three secretaries that worked here. I don't know why she would do such a thing, but I know she had some personal problems with her husband, Mike, who was a wife beater. He was arrested a few days ago, and I ordered Chief Barnes to keep him in jail, but he too was killed by the force within the rain." Mayor Anderson covered her body with an old blanket that Chief Barnes went and got for him.

"I'm sorry this happened, but we must now focus on the current situation," Chief Barnes said, touching the Mayor's shoulder. The man was still a little distraught over the situation before him. "I remember bringing him in, and I was ready to drop him off at his house, but the day he was supposed to go back home was the day he died." Chief Barnes explained while picking up the body with help from Johnny. They carried her into a back room; they figured they'd give her proper burial later, if they made it out alive. They made sure she was covered up well, and then they all met in the center room, and looked at each other and wondered what each one of them was thinking.

There was tension between all of them. They wondered if someone in the room was somehow behind this whole mess, but deep within themselves they all knew it was something unnatural outside waiting to get in and kill them all, but what was it? Johnny took Tracy's hand, and they walked into the other room to talk.

"What do you think is happening here?" Johnny asked nervously.

"I don't know, but I think we're all aware it's something weird going on. What do you think it could be?"

"I don't know, Tracy. But I have this feeling that it's somehow related to one of us," he said, looking into her eyes and hoping she would understand what he meant by that.

"One of us?"

"Yes, one of us!" Johnny said, trying to understand it himself, but he didn't have any answers either. "We'll just to have to keep an eye out for something unusual or someone acting weird. Okay?"

"I'll keep an eye out too. But we can't accuse anyone, even if they do act a little weird, because it could be just their way, that's all."

Johnny nodded, and they walked back into the main office, where everyone was discussing a way out and getting very irritated with each other and their. The night seemed still, as if time had forgotten Tucker Falls. The constant rain made everyone in the town hall depressed, because there was something about rain that made people very sad. Everyone felt a little cabin fever once in a while. The other residents of Tucker Falls remained secluded in their homes, and they locked their doors, hoping they were protected from the unknown force within the rain, but it only bought them time.

CHAPTER 9

DROPS OF BLOOD

Sonja Tucker was a librarian at the Tucker Falls Town Library. She was in her late fifties, and books were her thing, but she did once have an amazing thing happen to her—at least, she said it had happened. She'd been lying in bed one night a few years ago, and she'd had a heart attack and died and went to Heaven. Her vision of Heaven was gold, and everyone she knew that had died was very wealthy, but some said that she'd actually been fooled by Satan, because why would the Lord have gold in Heaven when the true riches were not gold, but love?

Many people thought she was crazy, and she never had a chance to prove her vision, but she vowed that she would see Heaven again.

"Yeah, when you die," one man said to her while she was telling her story to a gentleman in the library, and she told him to get out. She received an official warning for that outburst. Sonja was a beautiful person, though many people called her *Sonja Sightings,* from the hit Sci-Fi television show *Sightings*. She was never viewed as a real librarian, because of her vision.

She'd lived in Tucker Falls all her life, and she'd had a few boyfriends and had even been married once, for a year. Her husband had left her for a younger woman and they moved down to Miami, but a few years later, Sonja received a word that her ex-husband was killed in a car accident. They found six cans of Budweiser in the car, and he was not a person who could hold his booze.

Sonja was in the library fixing books, and she always enjoyed working there; it was her favorite thing to do because that's all she knew in her life. Without the library she wouldn't know what to do with herself. Maybe work in a factory? She enjoyed working in Tucker Falls, and that was that. It was after midnight, and she was probably the only person who worked late at night, but she was behind on some books. She did have the code to get in and out any time she wanted to, because she'd been there for all of her life and so they knew who she was and that she wouldn't steal from the library. Even though there had been a few books that had been misplaced in the last few years, but she always did her job.

It might not be wise for me to work so late, with all these murders taking place. But who would want to stay home and wait? I'd rather just be here alone to enjoy my books, and everyone else can leave me the hell alone! Sonja sat down to eat the ham sandwich she'd made before coming to the library. Like a writer who writes, an artist who paints, a salesperson who sells, or a wrestler who wrestles, Sonja was a librarian who took care of books. There were a lot of librarians out there who took real pride in their work; some just stuck to their jobs while others had outside hobbies or other activities, but in all cases they were all hard workers!

The library was big, even a little larger than the town hall itself. In some places, people thought the town hall should be bigger considering the circumstances, that the town hall was the capital of the village. In Tucker Falls that didn't matter, because there were a lot of people who were born in this small, busy town. Sonja enjoyed meeting new people that came into the library, because it was an option to be either a public or to a private person, and Sonja was happy to greet the public. Most people that drove through Tucker Falls stopped to look around, because the town itself was highly historical.

Sonja took a great pride in working for such a small, busy town. It was a pleasure; besides, when the locals teased her about her vision, she took the teasing calmly. In other circumstances she might get angry, but she felt the teasing was done with affection.

Boy, these books have some dust on them, and I can't believe people bring these books back late; especially teenagers who check 'em out and return them a month late. Either school is getting very demanding, or they're plain lazy. While eating her sandwich, Sonja decided to go home within fifteen minutes or so. Exhaustion was taking its toll on her, and she knew she wasn't going to last much longer if she stayed here and pushed herself to finish her work. She decided to finish checking in books that the other librarians didn't do, because they'd figured that Sonja would come in later and work some overtime.

Her normal hours were 11:00 a.m. to 4:00 p.m. She would sometimes go home and eat dinner, then come back, or she would stay late, but the issue was hers to settle and no one else's. She wasn't the supervisor—they'd given that job to a younger person, who hardly worked at the library. The supervisor was always taking off to see her boyfriend in Brunswick where she would spend the night with him every other day. The other librarians, including Sonja, were upset that Sonja didn't get the job four years back, but the town felt that Sonja would retire within seven years and they wanted someone younger, who would stick around for some time. But she wasn't as responsible as the others, especially Sonja, who always worked long hours and came in after midnight to finish things up. When Sonja found out she wasn't recognized as being a qualified applicant, she simply called out three days for sick time, and immersed herself within books to ease her pain.

The storm was getting worse as the night seemed to stand still, but how strange that the clocks in the town had all stopped! Ted's car was now covered with moss, as if it had been mounted in the ground, but the bodies were nowhere to be seen, and everyone in town stayed in their homes while the seven individuals remained trapped within town hall, awaiting their death sentences. They didn't know if there were weeks or months to wait, or if it was tonight!

CHAPTER 10

WANDA'S VISION

Wanda looked through the kitchen window of her apartment, and saw people outside trying to gather their luggage, as many were leaving town in an attempt to escape the evil that had settled on Tucker Falls. Many left pets behind in their rush, some figuring that the animals might serve as adequate sacrifice to the things within the rain. Other people believed that there were two killers, working together, but they didn't know the truth—except for Wanda, who was one of few who did know. People were getting soaked to their souls as they loaded their vehicles, looking for hope in another town, or hoping this whole mess would clear up soon enough, and they could return home. Wanda glared out through the window and wondered what was going to happen with her life. She had an interview in two days at MBNA America for a telemarketing position, which she had never done before, and the job paid $11 an hour for first shift. Wanda wanted to work the second shift: with differential, she'd earn another $1.69 an hour, plus benefits. The job was a regular Monday through Friday position, and some Saturdays, which sounded good to Wanda. She was hoping she would get good news after the interview.

Wanda got up from the kitchen table and walked into the living room. The lights in her apartment started to flicker. *Oh, please,* she thought, *don't lose power. God, I would hate to be left alone in the dark like that ice storm back in '98. Man, did that suck! I should get the candles from the glass cabinet and maybe light them, just in case.* Wanda went into her office looking for the candles she'd bought from the Dollar Store in Gray. She found them, and was looking for matches when the lights went out. She froze in her steps, holding the three candles in her shaky hands. She wondered when the power was going to be on, but needless to say, she was scared shitless. The power flickered on and off about five seconds apart, as if someone was playing with the light switch, but that wasn't the case. Wanda just stood there like a statue, waiting to see if the power would come back on. It didn't, and she was stuck in her apartment. She found the matches in the dark.

Wanda walked around a little as she wondered if CMP was doing anything about the power flickering. She reached the bedroom and she sat down slowly, putting the lit candle on the nightstand next to the bed. She got underneath the covers to go to sleep; it was past midnight, and it was time to go to bed and continue her job search in the morning. She hoped everything would go well with the interview the next day.

She started to doze off into dreamland, when suddenly there was a crash at her front door. She sat up quickly as if she had risen from the dead. She could hear gentle footsteps pattering in her kitchen. Wanda remained still, looking and listening for someone to come into her bedroom. The candle remained lit, and it threw shadows on the wall, including Wanda's. She couldn't move; then she heard footsteps coming toward the bedroom. *Please don't come in here. I didn't do anything wrong. I . . .* she remained still, sitting up in bed, holding her breath, and then . . . the candle blew out!

CHAPTER 11

Johnny And Tracy

Back in town hall, everyone remained calm as the wind started to pick up. They could hear screams throughout the town as if the shrieks were being amplified. Johnny and Tracy remained seated in one of the offices, and they heard the screams, too—the sounds of people in pain. Everyone inside the town hall knew that a lot of townspeople were getting killed by something in the rain, and there wasn't damn thing they could do about it.

"Man, why the hell did I come back to this crap hole?" Harley muttered. The relentless rain, pounding against the windows, and the wind swirling through the town hall, gave him an icy chill down his back. The wind was cold, and it was making it through the cracks of the old town hall, seeping through all of them like sweat going through pores. Harley wondered, why this town? And why are we still alive in town hall?

Johnny and Tracy asked themselves this very question, but no one knew the answer; except the rain people and they weren't talking. They all wondered what was going to happen to them, and what it would be like after this situation passed . . . if it did pass.

George glanced at the little girl with no name, who still didn't say a word. He wondered about her parents, and how he could find out who she was when she wouldn't talk. George wondered if she couldn't speak, but could still hear.

Mayor Anderson was asleep, dreaming of the past. He saw images of the town a long time ago, but only saw people shooting other people in the streets. There were three strangers walking the streets, carrying something in their hands, but they were in shadow, so Mayor Anderson couldn't make out who they were. He saw another man with him and he had a golden cross around his neck and soon, he realized that Harley was somehow related to Judge Holden. But how?

Johnny and Tracy dozed off as well, and they were dreaming of the same thing. Eventually, Harley was also in the land of dreams.

George, the little girl, and Chief Barnes were the only ones still awake, and Chief Barnes felt helpless staying in the town hall with his thumb up his ass. He watched the window, hearing screams in the night as the rain pounded buildings away with its fury of wind. The fog was gone, but it remained dark and time felt like it had stopped in place.

Three shadowed figures walked along the street, waving something at each house. At the end of the street, there were twelve tombstones; all were in good condition, considering the tombstones were made of wood. The three shadowy figures with no faces glanced upon the graves and they were waving something on the graves, but the sky was very dim and everything was a blur.

Johnny, Tracy, Mayor Anderson and Harley were all dreaming the same dream. One of the shadowy figures turned to them and smiled, and his teeth were covered with blood. His eyes were cherry red, as if filled with blood, but it was difficult to see his face past the gruesome grin. Then all of them woke up, and they were trying to gain their senses and wondered what they had just seen in their dreams.

"What happened?" Tracy asked, rubbing her eyes, which felt heavy and itchy. Tracy was still a little tired, but she wanted to stay awake and be with Johnny.

"I don't know," Johnny said, stretching his arms, feeling a little better after having a nap, disturbing as it was. "I had a weird dream about three guys with no faces, but one of them turned and looked at me with bloody eyes, and his teeth were covered with blood as if he were a vampire, but then I woke up," Johnny said.

Tracy looked him with wide eyes, realizing Johnny was describing the same dream she'd had. "What did the dream mean?" Tracy asked.

"I don't know, but I think it's something to do with what's going on right now in the rain—and perhaps in the whole town," Johnny said, holding Tracy's hand while thinking and looking around the old wooden office.

Johnny and Tracy talked about the situation, and realized that maybe the dream and the rain were somehow related, but they couldn't figure out how. They got up, and walked through town hall, stepping over tiny cracks in the floor where the old wood was rotting away like a piece of paper that melts within minutes after making contact with water. Thunder was in the background as the whole building shook, suddenly waking everyone up. Items fell off the desks and pictures dropped off the walls, smashing the glass to pieces.

"Look! There's something moving around out there!" George shouted, his face glued to the window by the mayor's office. They all gathered near the window like a bunch of spectators watching an unexpected event unfold.

"What the hell is that moving around in the rain?" Mayor Anderson said, watching figures resembling people walking around the rain, but it was still too dark to tell what they were, exactly. The rain was bouncing off things that were moving. Chief Barnes looked on, thinking that somebody might be outside looking for shelter before being discovered by the something within the rain, but he had his doubts still.

George felt the same way. "We must go outside and try to help those people! Maybe they're lost or something? Let's help," George said loudly, staring out the window as if in a trance.

"We don't know what the hell is out there," the mayor said emphatically.

"The mayor's right. We should stay here for our safety," Johnny suggested, his arms still wrapped around Tracy, holding her tightly to him.

"We should go out there and help them," the little girl said with a voice so low and sweet it grabbed everyone's attention. They all turned to look at her, especially George, who felt like a father to the girl, because he'd found her standing in the rain and had taken her in.

"You talked, little girl!" George said, kneeling in front of her with a sigh of relief at knowing she was able to speak. "How come you didn't say anything before?" George was genuinely happy that she was talking.

"I was afraid of you and everyone. That's all," she said in a voice as soft as cotton.

"What's your name?" George said.

The little girl looked at him. "My name is Brandi Williamson," she said.

"That's a lovely name, Brandi," George said softly, looking around wondering how she'd gotten a doll suddenly. "Where did you get that doll, Brandi?"

"I found it in a closet, in the office over there," she said, stroking the doll's silky hair that still had dust on it. George looked at the doll, then turned and looked at Mayor Anderson with a blank stare. He rose slowly, keeping his eyes on the mayor and walked over to the man, his eyes filling with fire and his fists clenched tightly, ready to strike.

"You BASTARD! I'm going to kill you!" George shouted, drawing back his arm to throw a punch. Chief Barnes stepped in quickly and grabbed George, forcing him back to the wall. George struggled, trying to get to the mayor who was shivering a little, unsure of what George knew.

"Now, relax. What the hell is the matter with you?" Chief Barnes asked while Harley, Johnny, and Tracy watched with questioning looks on their faces.

"He's the one! That bastard!"

Chief Barnes took George down to the floor and pinned him there until he stopped struggling. Mayor Anderson's face was suddenly filled with fear as he kept his distance from George and Chief Barnes.

"I know what he's talking about," the mayor said, hoping not to make a mess in his pants. "That doll she's holding was George's sister's, but she was killed in a car accident. I was the one driving the car that killed her ten years ago." Mayor Anderson looked at everyone, who was staring back at the mayor, wondering what he was saying. "I was driving that car and his little sister was eight at the time. I was driving drunk, and I missed the curve in Durham and I drove off the road, killing her. I suffered a broken leg and a couple of broken ribs, and I told the police that a deer came out in front of me and I'd swerved to avoid it. But that wasn't the case at all. When I crashed, Judy was still alive, and there was a bottle of alcohol in the car. If I was caught, I would've been thrown in jail and I would have never had become mayor of Tucker Falls. So I left her." Mayor Anderson looked nervous as he told his story, wondering what the others would do to him, now that his secret was out.

"I'm sorry, George, for everything, but there's another side to this story—" A window crashed in the lobby area, and Chief Barnes and George ran over to see what had happened. They saw something coming through the doorway, but it stopped and slowly turned its dark, glassy face toward the two men and growled like a tiger.

"What the hell is that?" George asked. Chief Barnes was stunned by the hideous demon that had appeared in front of them.

"I don't know, but it sure isn't natural," Chief Barnes said in a shaky voice, backing up closer to the lobby. He could see other figures out there walking around with something in their claws, but he couldn't make it out what they were holding.

"Man, we're in a lot of shit! Aren't we, chief?" George said. The others came around the corner of the hallway to see if everything was all right.

The rain started to come down like rocks hitting cars, but this was no picnic on a mountain; there was something evil out in the rain.

I've seen some crazy shit, but I've never seen anything like this in my entire life. Why didn't the creature come in like it wanted to? Something stopped it in its tracks, but what? The chief didn't know what to do. He wanted to know what it was that was trying to get into the town hall, and what had stopped it. Johnny and Tracy wondered the same, but Johnny had a profound anger at the rain; his parents had been slaughtered by the beasts, or creatures, or whatever they were. George remained enraged at the mayor, who had never finished the story of what had happened to his sister. The mayor looked at George, knowing he was in trouble, and he wondered if he should tell the whole story, or just leave things as they were.

Tracy's screams interrupted all of their thoughts. Something had grabbed her from outside, and it was trying to pull her out into the rain. Everyone ran to assist her; she was almost through the window and then George got ahold of her ankles, and he started to pull. Whatever it was that had Tracy let her go and seized George, hauling him through the window like a piece of paper being sucked up by a vacuum. There were no screams—George was gone, and he had saved Tracy's life. The mayor was somewhat relieved, but he was also upset because he lost an old friend.

"What the hell just happened?" The chief asked loudly, looking out through the window while Johnny hugged Tracy tight.

"Something grabbed me through the window. I didn't hear anything, and then all at once something caught me, but I don't know what," she said, catching her breath. Chief Barnes was furious that he wasn't there sooner to help. The mayor kept his distance while the little girl stared at him with a quizzical look, as if she knew what he was thinking. The mayor went into his office and closed the door, locking it. The mayor sat at his desk while the others tried to find a solution to the problem that surrounded them.

"I think I know what the problem is here."

Harley looked at everyone and then turned his head toward one of the windows in the lobby.

"What do you mean? You know what the problem is?" Johnny said with confusion.

"Yes, my friend. The problem lies with me . . . and with someone else here, too." Harley fixed his stare on Johnny. "The problem is the mayor and me. And what I mean by that is . . . that we are the last of our kind." Harley turned back to gaze out into the dark mist outside.

"What do you mean, 'the last of your kind'?" Chief Barnes asked.

"A long time ago—a few hundred years ago—the townspeople of Tucker Falls executed twelve criminals. Their graves were blessed, but the three priests that blessed those graves were also found guilty, of using witchcraft. They were burned alive!" Harley explained, trying to catch his breath because the truth was disturbing to reveal.

"How do you know? And why didn't you come forward with this earlier?" Chief Barnes asked while staring at Harley, trying to decide if he was telling the truth or not.

"Who would believe me about that situation? I mean, it's a crazy story about three dead priests who were burned at the stake for doing witchcraft three centuries ago. But it wasn't true—they were only doing the Lord's work. "Mayor Anderson was a long distance relative, like cousins and our ancestor was Judge Holden. Johnnny and Tracy's ancestors were the one's that did this along with Judge Holden. This is why *they have come back*. The mayor and I are the last two remaining ancestors of Judge Holden. Those things out there—they're coming for us."

A hush flew through the building, and then there was a booming knock at the door.

"It's them! They're trying to come in," Harley said. A noise made him turn around. He saw Brandi, the little girl, start to grow tall. Her limbs stretched, and she was no longer human but a creature of some sort, and there was a necklace with a cross around her neck covered with stained moss. The creature reached out toward Harley, but the chief jumped the creature. It knocked the chief to the floor. Johnny tried next, but he was flung into the wall by the creature's great strength. Harley just stood there as the creature approached him. The monster was covered with moss, but Harley could just make out a priest's outfit underneath. It grabbed Harley, but he held up his necklace that had the golden cross on it with Jesus. The creature stared at Harley with its burning sun eyes, and it backed away. It spun, and then leapt toward the mayor's office. Mayor Anderson's screams of terror could be heard above the ripping sounds, as if the mayor was being torn apart. A moment later, the creature walked through the door holding the mayor's head in its right claw. Its eyes flashed as it looked at the people and it said in an otherworldly, dark voice: "BE TRUE, BE TRUE OR DIE!"

Then the creature walked out through the lobby doors and into the rain. When the sun rose moments later to dry the land, peace was throughout Tucker Falls and the rain was gone.

Harley, Johnny, and Tracy walked out the front doors. They looked up and saw one cloud in the distance; and it was dark cloud, a reminder that this could happen again.

About the Author

Duane E. Coffill was born on September 4, 1973 in Brunswick, Maine. He grew up in Freeport, Maine and graduated from Freeport High School in 1992. He started writing at the age of twelve.

He has been to Andover College (Kaplan University), US Career Institute and Full Sail University for computer and writing classes. At the age of nineteen, he was diagnosed with Crohn's Disease. He was saved in 1996 and loves the Lord Jesus Christ.

Since then, he has written many stories and poems. He is the founder/President of Horror Writers Of Maine and Horror Authors Alliance. He is a proud member of the New England Horror Writers.

He currently resides in Windham, Maine with his beautiful wife, Shelley and he sees his two beautiful daughters, Madelyn and Savannah bi-weekly. He is currently working on two novels and three short stories.

Made in the USA
Middletown, DE
03 July 2016